The Sleepover Club

Three fantastic Sleepover Club stories in one!

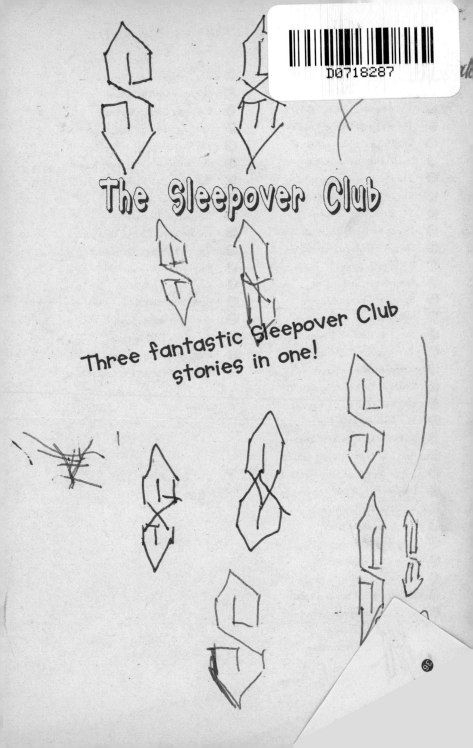

Have you been invited to all these Sleepovers?

1. The Sleepover Club at Frankie's
2. The Sleepover Club at Lyndsey's
3. The Sleepover Club at Felicity's
4. The Sleepover Club at Rosie's
5. The Sleepover Club at Kenny's
6. Starring The Sleepover Club
7. The Sleepover Girls go Spice
8. The 24-Hour Sleepover Club
9. The Sleepover Club Sleeps Out
10. Happy Birthday, Sleepover Club
11. Sleepover Girls on Horseback
12. Sleepover in Spain
13. Sleepover on Friday 13th
14. Sleepover Girls go Camping
15. Sleepover Girls go Detective
16. Sleepover Girls Go Designer
17. The Sleepover Club Surfs the Net
18. Sleepover Girls on Screen
19. Sleepover Girls and Friends
20. Sleepover Girls on the Catwalk
21. The Sleepover Club Goes for Goal!
22. Sleepover Girls go Babysitting
23. Sleepover Girls go Snowboarding
24. Happy New Year, Sleepover Club!
25. Sleepover Club 2000
26. We Love You Sleepover Club
27. Vive le Sleepover Club!
28. Sleepover Eggstravaganza
29. Emergency Sleepover
30. Sleepover Girls on the Range
31. The Sleepover Club Bridesmaids
32. Sleepover Girls see Stars
33. Sleepover Club Blitz
34. Sleepover Girls in the Ring
35. Sari Sleepover
36. Merry Christmas Sleepover Club!
37. The Sleepover Club Down Under
38. Sleepover Girls go Splash!
39. Sleepover Girls go Karting
40. Sleepover Girls go Wild!
41. The Sleepover Club at the Carnival
42. The Sleepover Club on the Beach
43. Sleepover Club Vampires
44. sleepoverclub.com
45. Sleepover Girls go Dancing
46. The Sleepover Club on the Farm
47. Sleepover Girls go Gymtastic!
48. Sleepover Girls on the Ball
49. Sleepover Club Witches
50. Sleepover Club Ponies
51. Sleepover Girls on Safari
52. Sleepover Club Makeover
53. Sleepover Girls go Surfing
54. Sleepover Girls go Treasure Hunting

Mega
Sleepover Club ①

The Sleepover Club at Frankie's
The Sleepover Club at Lyndsey's
The Sleepover Club at Felicity's

Rose Impey

Collins
An imprint of HarperCollinsPublishers

The Sleepover Club ® is a registered trademark of HarperCollins*Publishers* Ltd

The Sleepover Club at Frankie's first published in Great Britain by Collins 1997
The Sleepover Club at Lyndsey's first published in Great Britain by Collins 1997
The Sleepover Club at Felicity's first published in Great Britain by Collins 1997

First published in this three-in-one edition by Collins 2002

Collins is an imprint of HarperCollins*Publishers* Ltd
77-85 Fulham Palace Road, Hammersmith
London W6 8JB

The HarperCollins*Children'sBooks* website address is
www.harpercollinschildrensbooks.co.uk

6

Text copyright © Rose Impey 1997
Original series characters, plotlines and settings © Rose Impey 1997

ISBN 0 00 710902 4

The authors assert the moral right to be identified as the authors of the work.

Printed and bound in England by Clays Ltd, St Ives plc

Sleepover Kit List

1. Sleeping bag
2. Pillow
3. Pyjamas or a nightdress
4. Slippers
5. Toothbrush, toothpaste, soap etc
6. Towel
7. Teddy
8. A creepy story
9. Food for a midnight feast:
   chocolate, crisps, sweets, biscuits.
   In fact anything you like to eat.
10. Torch
11. Hairbrush
12. Hair things like a bobble or hairband,
    if you need them
13. Clean knickers and socks
14. Change of clothes for the next day
15. Sleepover diary and membership card

Mrs Flood

The Sleepover Club at Frankie's

A BOYFRIEND FOR BROWN OWL

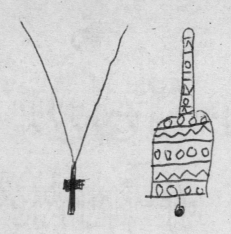

CHAPTER ONE

Well, come in, if you're coming in. And sit down. This time we're in deep trouble. This time we could be in doom for ever. And this time it was *not* my idea. Uh-oh! There's the phone.

"Frankie! It's for you."

"Coming, Mum."

You'd better come down and listen in. I've got a feeling this could be *bad* news.

"Hello?"

"Frankie, is that you?"

"No, it's Betty Boop."

"Look, be serious for once. Has Brown Owl been round to your house?"

"No! Why?"

"She's been here already, so you'd better look out."

"What happened? Go on, tell me the worst."

"I can't, my mum's coming. I've been grounded and that includes the phone."

"Oh, help, Kenny! I think she's at the door now. What should I do?"

"Hide. Run away. Emigrate. But disappear!"

Come on. 5-4-3-2-1, let's get gone! Upstairs, quick!

Right, close that door. On second thoughts, lock it, we don't want to be disturbed. This is seriously serious. What do you think she'll tell them? Oh, p-lease, not everything! I mean, we haven't done anything terrible. It's not as if we *meant* to wreck the supermarket. We were just trying to be helpful, which is what she's always telling us Brownies are supposed to be.

I blame Rosie. None of this would have happened if we hadn't let her join the Sleepover Club. That was the start of it all. Oh, flipping Ada, as my grandma says, pull up a pew. I suppose I'd better tell you exactly what happened.

To begin with there were just the four of us.

There was me, Francesca Thomas. But you can call me Frankie.

And there was Laura McKenzie. We call her Kenny. She's my best friend. That doesn't mean we never fall out – we argue at least once a day – but we always make it up.

And Fliss. Her real name's Felicity Sidebotham, but please don't bother with the jokes, she's heard them all before. And, as everybody knows, Fliss doesn't have much of a sense of humour.

And Lyndsey Collins. Now *she* does. Lyndz is a great laugh.

So that's how it *used* to be.

Now there's Rosie as well, which, in case you can't count, makes five.

Rosie's only recently moved round here; she doesn't know many people yet, so we thought we'd be friendly. OK, we were curious as well. She'd moved into that big house at the end of Welby Drive, the one with the massive garden with an orchard, so we were expecting someone really posh. But Rosie is not posh. Up to now we haven't been inside, but we're working on it.

It was Lyndsey who suggested we let Rosie sit with us in class and hang around with us at dinner, which was cool with us, but then, the next thing, she said, "I think we should let Rosie join the Sleepover Club."

I said, "What for?" as if I needed to ask.

"Well, I feel sorry for her; she's got no

friends." Lyndz is the sort of person that would rescue a fly if it fell in a puddle.

"That's not our problem," said Fliss. "Anyway it would make five and five's an odd number and odd numbers never work." Fliss likes everything to be tidy. She even lifts hairs off your cardigan while she's talking to you.

But for once I agreed with her. "We don't really know her, do we? She might be a drip. She might be a scaredy cat. She might be really boring."

"She's not," said Lyndz. "She passed the test, didn't she?"

I suppose she did. We wouldn't even have let her hang around with us at school otherwise. We do these naughty things: you know, like screwing up paper pellets and stuffing them down the back of the art cupboard to feed Muriel, our pretend pet monster. Sometimes we tie one of us to a tree behind the mobile classroom, then knock on the door and run away. If you want to be in the gang you have to do a dare and get sent to Mrs Poole's office. We dared Rosie to take a bite out of a biscuit in the teachers' tin on the staff-room table and then put it back. She ate half the biscuit, so we had to let her join. But there's something about her I'm still not sure about.

"Well, I don't care who joins," said Kenny, "as long as we have a laugh."

"But she doesn't laugh, that's the trouble," I said. "She's a bit of a sad case, really."

"That's because her dad's left," said Lyndz.

"So's mine," said Fliss.

"Yes, but you've got another one," Kenny pointed out.

"Andy is not my dad," Fliss insisted.

We argued for ages until Fliss said, "Let's stop bickering and have a vote and settle it once and for all." She can be so bossy sometimes. "Those in favour."

Lyndz and Kenny put up their hands.

"Those against."

Me and Fliss put up ours.

"Oh, well, that really settles it," I said. "Now what do we do?"

Well, we didn't do anything, until the following week when we were all at Brownies. We were sitting on the wall outside, waiting for Kenny's dad to pick us up. We were talking about our next sleepover, which was at my house the following weekend. Just then Rosie came over, because she's started Brownies too.

"I've got these really cute Forever Friends jimjams," Fliss was telling us. "You'll see them at the sleepover on Saturday."

"What's that?" asked Rosie.

Suddenly everyone went quiet. Kenny started to whistle, which she always does when she's nervous. I looked at my feet, which are pretty fascinating. No, really, they are, because they're the biggest feet

15

you've ever seen. I take size sixes already. Of course I'm tall for my age and, as my mum says, if I didn't have big feet I'd be for ever falling over. Fliss sucked her cheeks in, which is a silly habit and makes her look like a gerbil. Then, out of the blue, we all heard Lyndz say, "Oh, it's our Sleepover Club. It's at Frankie's house on Friday. Do you want to come?"

After Rosie had gone, Fliss turned on her and said, "Why did you say that?"

But she needn't have asked. We all said together, "*Because she felt sorry for her!*"

So that was it. Thanks to big-hearted Lyndsey, with a mouth to match, we now had five in the Sleepover Club.

CHAPTER TWO

Of course that was only part of it. The other person I blame is Fliss. If she wasn't so potty about weddings, we definitely wouldn't be in this mess now. And I wouldn't be sitting here, hiding in my bedroom from Brown Owl.

Fliss is so potty about weddings that she even marries her toys. Whenever you go round to her house, there's a rabbit in a wedding dress or a teddy wearing a veil or a Barbie getting married to a My Little Pony. She reads a bit out of the Bible, plays a tune on the keyboard and then she says, "And now you may kiss the bride." Then they get to sit together on a shelf in their wedding clothes living happily ever after.

That's how she came up with her bright idea. "Why don't we have a wedding at our next sleepover?" she said, dead excited.

"*A wedding*?" I said.

"Yeah. I could be the bride, and you could be the groom."

"Why me?"

"Because you've got a boy's name."

"So's Kenny."

"You're the tallest. Kenny can be bridesmaid. You'll have to wear a dress, though," she told Kenny, "you can't wear your soccer strip."

I said, "Dream on!"

Kenny grinned and sat there shaking her head. Kenny lives and dies in her football top. She's devoted to Leicester City football team and just about everything she wears has got The Fox's logo on it. Me and Kenny have been friends since playschool and I have never seen her in a frilly frock.

"Anyway," I said, "you can forget it. I'm not marrying anybody."

"I'll marry you," Lyndz said.

"Brillo," said Fliss and gave Lyndz a hug.

So we worked it all out: Kenny would be best man and I'd be the vicar. I'd borrow a white cotton nightie of my mum's and Fliss's Bible and an old pair of Dad's glasses. All my toys and Pepsi, our dog, would be the guests and we'd do it out in the garden. All we were short of was a bridesmaid, so, at the time, it seemed quite lucky that Rosie joined the Sleepover Club when she did.

Lyndz has an excellent set of dressing-up clothes that used to be her mum's. She brought Fliss an old wedding dress and a net curtain for a veil; she found a soldier's outfit for herself to wear, and painted on a moustache. There was a pink fairy dress that Rosie wore, and Kenny wore her soccer strip with a jacket over the top.

We all had to hum the "Here comes the bride" tune and then Lyndz and Fliss walked down my garden path through the arch where the roses used to grow, before Pepsi dug them up. Arm in arm.

I started off, "We are gathered here," and then I rambled on till everyone started to look bored. I didn't say the bit about "And now you may kiss the bride" because Lyndz had made me promise to leave it out. But we did the bit where they exchange rings. And then we took lots of photos. Pepsi got too excited and kept running off with the other guests in her mouth, so in the end we had to lock her in the house.

At last we got to the best bit: the food. We had veggie hot dogs, popcorn, crisp-

and-banana sandwiches, marshmallows, lemon jelly, and chocolate fudge cake. Sometimes, when we've finished, we get a big salad bowl and mix all the leftovers together, hot dogs, crisps, jelly, the lot, and stir it up until it looks like a dog's dinner. We call it Nappy's Brains. We call it that because there's a boy called Nathan, who lives next door to me, who we call Nappyhead, because he's really stupid. But don't let me get started on that subject or I'll never finish this story.

Usually we dare someone to eat it. I looked round and chose Kenny.

"I dare you," I said to her.

"I double dare you," she said to me.

"I triple dare you," I said to her.

"Oh, that's not fair," said Lyndz. "It's always Kenny has to do it."

"All right, I dare Rosie," I said.

Everyone went quiet because they thought it was mean to dare Rosie when she was still new. But I don't see what difference that makes. Anyway she picked up the spoon and ate two heaped spoonfuls. We all collapsed on the floor gagging and pretending to be sick, but she just rolled her eyes and looked at us as if we were really weird. So that was another test she'd passed.

After that it was time to go to bed. I've got quite a big bedroom with a bed *and* a set of bunks in it. And we've got a camp bed. So, when the sleepover's at mine, all four of us can fit in.

You see, I'm an only child, which is a very sore point in my house. I've just about given up trying to persuade my parents to have another baby, but I still don't like it. They don't seem to realise what a disadvantage it is to grow up an only child. So I think the least they can do is make it up to me by letting me have my friends round to stay whenever I want, which they usually do. So that's pretty coo-el.

But there wasn't a bed for Rosie, so Kenny and I had to share my bed. This seemed like a great idea until she got the giggles and the fidgets, which always happens with Kenny. She also has the most freezing feet in the world!

Because Rosie is new, she doesn't have a sleepover kit like the rest of us, so Felicity showed her what she needed to get. We all have a bag and in it is:

1. Sleeping bag
2. Pillow
3. Pyjamas or a nightdress, but they're draughty and fly up and show your bottom when you do gymnastics
4. Slippers
5. Toothbrush, toothpaste, soap etc
6. Towel
7. Teddy
8. A creepy story

9. Food for a midnight feast:
   chocolate, crisps, sweeties,
   biscuits and any other yummy
   foods you can bring.
10. A torch
11. Hairbrush
12. Hair things like a bobble or
    hairband, if you need them
13. Clean knickers and socks. And a
    smelly bag for old ones!
14. Sleepover diary

For the wedding:
15. Wedding clothes
16. Camera
17. Confetti

We all keep a diary. Sometimes we read each other bits out of them, but they are *absolutely private*, on pain of death! We would never look in each other's without permission. We write all our secret secrets in them. If you haven't got any secrets, you can make them up. At least, that's what I do.

I wrote in mine: *When I grow up I don't want to be a pop star any more. I want to drive a taxi.*

I went in a taxi for the first time last week when we went to London. It was class.

Kenny was writing loads in hers, all about what she'd learned about how babies are made. She read it out to us. Kenny's going to be a doctor, like her dad, when she grows up. She says you have to be really tough to be a doctor. She loves anything with blood in it. And she knows all about babies and things. She wrote: *I'm not going to have a baby, though. And I'm not getting married. I shall be far too busy saving lives.*

Felicity started to giggle. "I am," she said. "I'm going to marry Ryan Scott and have lots of children and run a playgroup."

Ryan Scott is a boy in our class. Kenny made a being-sick noise.

I said, "He's the saddest thing on earth."

"Boys smell," said Lyndz, wrinkling her nose. And Lyndz has four brothers, so she should know.

"How do you like boys?" I asked Rosie.

"In a sandwich," she said, "with tomato ketchup and chips on the side."

"Yeah! good one," I said.

Suddenly thinking about chips made us all feel hungry. It wasn't midnight yet, but we decided to have our midnight feast. I sneaked downstairs to get a big bowl and we put everything in it. There was fizzy rock, Black Jacks, Fruit Salads, chewy dinosaurs, jelly babies, a Snickers bar, and a bag of cheese and onion crisps. We passed it round and started talking about Brownies.

"It's no fun any more," said Kenny.

It's true. It used to be supercool, but it's boring these days.

"Brown Owl's always in a razz."

"She used to be really nice," said Lyndz.

"It's because she's fallen out with her boyfriend," said Fliss. "Auntie Jill told me." Fliss's Auntie Jill is Snowy Owl, that's how she knows so much. "She told my mum Brown Owl might give up running Brownies because she just doesn't feel interested in anything any more."

"That's a shame," said Lyndsey. "I feel—"

"*Really sorry for her*!" we all chimed in.

"Well, I do! It's horrid when somebody gets dumped."

"You should see my mum," said Rosie. "Since my dad left, she looks much happier."

But you could tell by the way she said it that Rosie wasn't happy. We knew she was missing her dad, but we didn't know what to say to cheer her up.

It was half past twelve and there was

nothing left to eat. We were lying in the dark with our torches on, starting to get dozy. We were trying hard to stay awake. After all, the whole idea of sleepover is *not* to go to sleep.

Lyndz is always the first to drop off. We could hear her sucking her thumb. Then Fliss started sniffing, which she always does, so Kenny and I played pass the sniff. We do it at school in silent reading, it drives Mrs Weaver mad. Then Rosie joined in, which made me and Kenny giggle. Suddenly Kenny sat up in bed. She'd had this idea.

"Why don't we find her a *new* boyfriend?" she said.

"Who?" said Rosie.

"Brown Owl, of course."

"How would we do that?" I said. I meant, where would you look? There isn't exactly a shop to go to.

"Well, there must be someone out there," said Kenny.

"Mmm," Rosie agreed.

I was just dropping off, which is the time when I get most of my brilliant ideas. "What about Dishy Dave?" I said, yawning.

"Who's Dishy Dave?" said Rosie.

But I was too tired to explain. "Tell you ... in the... morn... ing," I said, and fell asleep.

CHAPTER THREE

We usually wake up in the opposite order to the way we go to sleep. Lyndz is always awake first and once *she's* awake, everyone's awake. She's the noisiest person alive. She was sleeping on the camp bed and every time she moved, it squeaked. And when she leant over to reach for her sleepover bag, the camp bed collapsed at one end and catapulted her out on the floor.

So she woke us all up squealing and giggling. The next thing, she'd got the hiccups. When Lyndz gets hiccups, she really gets hiccups. She could get in the *Guinness Book of Records* for hiccups.

We've tried all sorts of ways of curing her of them: a cold key down her back, giving her a fright, standing on her head – No, not us standing on her head! – wet flannels, pinching her nose, making her sing "God Save the Queen" backwards. But best of all is pressing down hard with your thumbs on the palm of her hand, while she holds her breath.

But the minute you wake up in the morning is not a time when your brain is working well. So it took a bit longer than usual, and the longer the hiccups went on, the pinker Lyndz's face got and the more she hiccuped. In the end I managed it with my magic thumbs, but some people are never grateful.

"That really hurt," she complained, rubbing her hand.

"Oh, tell me about it," I said. I thought my thumbs would never recover. Then I tripped over the camp bed, which folded under me, so I ended up on the floor too.

Lyndz made the mistake of laughing. OK, I thought, *payback time*! And I picked up Stanley, who is my toughest bear.

Teddy fights are one of our favourite things. Sometimes we use pillows, but the best fights are with squishy-poos. A squishy-poo is a sleeping bag filled with clothes and things, which you whack each other with while balancing on a bed. That's one of our International Gladiator events. But you need plenty of room for that.

When it's a teddy fight, Stanley always wins because he's stuffed really hard and he's quite big. You can see the other bears tremble when they see him coming. Stanley is unbeatable.

I could see Rosie watching us again, thinking *definitely weird*. But she'll get used to us in time. Then my dad came in, so we had to stop.

"When you've quite finished the demolition job, it's time for breakfast," he said.

While we were getting ready, Rosie said, "Now tell me who Dishy Dave is."

"You know, he's the new caretaker at school," said Fliss, butting in before I could speak. "Dave's great."

He is great. He used to drive a mobile library van before he came to our school. He's quite young and we all like him because he doesn't tell us off. He's really nice to the infants. Sometimes, if they offer him a cup of tea, he sits down in the home corner with a crown on his head and pretends to be Prince Charles. He's a good laugh.

"Isn't he married?"

"I don't think so," said Fliss. "Why?"

"He could go out with Brown Owl," Rosie suggested.

"What a brilliant idea!" said Fliss "Why didn't I think of that?"

"Probably because I thought of it first," I said.

"It was my idea," Kenny muttered.

"Rosie thought of it, actually," said Fliss.

"How would you know?" I said. "You were asleep, *actually*!"

Things could have got difficult. Me and Fliss often get into arguments about who thought of something first, but then my mum called us for breakfast so that was that.

But whoever's idea it was, it spelled t-r-o-u-b-l-e. And we'd have been better off if nobody had thought of it. But you know Fliss, once she gets hold of an idea she won't let go, especially if it's got anything to do with weddings.

"Just think," she said, "they might fall in love and get married. I bet Brown Owl would be so grateful, she'd even let us be her bridesmaids."

"I doubt it," I said.

Kenny rolled her eyes. She doesn't mind dressing up for a laugh, but she wouldn't want to be a bridesmaid. Personally, I wouldn't mind, if I could choose what I wore. I'm really into silver. I've got a pair of silver shoes and occasionally, at weekends, I'm allowed to wear silver nail varnish. The others sometimes call me Spaceman. But I couldn't see Brown Owl wanting bridesmaids dressed in silver.

I said, "Knowing Brown Owl, she'd probably make us wear our Brownie uniforms."

"But we'd still get to go to her wedding," said Fliss.

"I think it's a great idea," said Lyndz. "It'd be nice for both of them."

"Come on, let's make a plan," said Felicity.

"I think we'd better find out if he's already got a girlfriend first," I said.

"How will we do that?" said Rosie.

"We'll ask him," said Kenny.

"When?"

"On Monday," I said. "The sooner the better."

CHAPTER FOUR

We all go to the same school. It's called Cuddington County Primary and it's a great school. Our teacher's called Mrs Weaver and she's great too, so's the Head, Mrs Poole. She never shouts, she just looks disappointed with you, if you get sent to her. It's not so bad, as long as you keep looking at your feet.

There's only one thing wrong with our school and that's Mrs Pickett; she's one of the dinner ladies. Mrs Pickernose, we call her. She does nothing but tell people off. She is bad news. But apart from her, we all like our school.

Dishy Dave is what we call Mr Driver. That's because he's dead tall and good-looking, a bit like Brad Pitt. And he's a good laugh. He calls us 'guys' and the boys 'girls'. He kicks a football around with them sometimes and he plays the piano for us to dance to; he knows all sorts of tunes.

Practising our dance routines is one of our best skives. We go into the studio and turn all the lights off, apart from one or two spots, and pretend we're dancers with Oasis. Or sometimes we go in the hall to dance and Mr Driver plays the piano. If the M&Ms haven't got there first, that is. The M&Ms are our biggest enemies – Emma Hughes and Emily Berryman, yuk! – but I'll tell you about them another time.

Mr Driver lives just down the road from school and he's always in and out. The only time he's too busy to talk to you is at home time, when he has to get on with the cleaning, but apart from that he never minds a good old chat.

So, on Monday, we went looking for him at break time. We found him cleaning some graffiti off the side of one of the mobile classrooms. We sidled up to him and then hung around waiting for the right moment.

"Uh-oh," he said, "here comes trouble." But he smiled and went on scrubbing. "This wasn't your handiwork, I suppose?"

"Nooo!" we said. "Certainly not!" And we all looked as if butter wouldn't melt in our mouths, as my grandma says.

After a bit I said, "Dave..." He doesn't mind us calling him Dave.

"Have you got a girlfriend?"

He stopped scrubbing and started to grin. "No. But I think I'm a bit old for you, don't you?"

I went bright red. The others started to laugh as if it was *so* funny.

"She didn't mean that," said Fliss. "We

were just interested. Have you really not got a girlfriend?"

"Nope," he said.

"Would you like one?" said Lyndz.

"Nope," he said. "Too much trouble."

"No, seriously," said Kenny.

Mr Driver sort of narrowed his eyes at us. "Why are you asking?"

"We could find you one, if you like," I said.

"What's the catch?"

We all said, "There is no catch."

"In that case I'd like Pamela Anderson."

"Don't be silly," said Fliss. "We don't know Pamela Anderson."

"Sorry, not interested, then," he said. "I'm saving myself for Pamela."

And he went back to scrubbing *Wiggie woz here* off the back of the mobile. Then the whistle went for the end of break. We shrugged and sort of drifted off.

"Do you think he was serious?" said Felicity.

"Oh, get a life," I said.

"Course he wasn't serious," said Lyndz.

"Where's he ever going to meet Pamela Anderson?" said Kenny.

"Even so," I said, not feeling very hopeful, "I doubt if he's going to settle for Brown Owl."

I wasn't being horrible about Brown Owl. She's very nice. She's quite pretty, with dark eyes and shoulder-length brown hair, and she looks really smart in her uniform. But Pamela Anderson she is not. She works in Barclays Bank and sometimes when I go in with my mum she's behind the counter and she smiles at us. She wears glasses at work and they really suit her but she doesn't wear them all the time. She's got a nice smile and a good sense of humour. Or she had. But she looks like a real wet weekend these days. It wasn't only Lyndsey who felt sorry for her, we all did.

But feeling sorry wasn't enough. We needed action, and action was our speciality! We decided to call it Operation Blind Date, or OBD for short. That was Felicity's idea! She even wanted us to write to Cilla Black to get Dave and Brown Owl on the show, but fortunately that was one of Fliss's bright ideas we decided against.

CHAPTER FIVE

Hang on a minute. Was that the phone? Quick, let's go and listen at the top of the stairs. Careful, my door squeaks. If my mum hears us, I'm in real doom.

"Hello... No, Felicity, you can't talk to Francesca... no, I'm sorry, she can't call you back... because Francesca is grounded... I haven't decided how long for. Possibly for ever...

"Yes, I'll tell her you rang..."

Uh-oh. If my mum's calling me Francesca, it must be serious. I wish I knew what Brown Owl's been saying. Do you suppose she's told them about Kenny and Rosie and the shopping-trolley incident? Or even worse, she might have told them about the letter. Which letter? The letter we sent Dishy Dave from Brown Owl, of course. That was *definitely not* my idea. I knew from the beginning *that* was a mistake.

But the problem was, we needed to get Dave and Brown Owl together and it wasn't going to be easy. As far as we knew they'd never even set eyes on each other. But we had to start somewhere, so we decided to start with Dave.

Every time he saw us around school he kept on asking us if there was any word from Pamela yet, and telling us he was keeping Saturday free, and other silly things. So we decided we'd tell him about this person we knew, this grown-up friend of ours called Madeline, who really wanted to meet him.

We didn't tell him she was our Brown Owl. As Kenny said, someone who wants to go out with Pamela Anderson might not be interested if he knows she runs the Brownies.

"So, what's this *friend* like?" he asked.

"Nice," we all said in chorus.

He rolled his eyes. "What does she do?"

"She works in a bank," said Felicity. That seemed OK.

"How old is she?"

"About your age," said Kenny, quick as a flash. Dave didn't look convinced.

"She's got her own car," I said. He seemed impressed by that.

Then he asked us what she looked like. OK, so perhaps we exaggerated a bit, but like my grandma says, beauty is in the eye of the beholder.

We got stuck when he asked us what music she was into. We hadn't a clue.

"Blur, Oasis, I think," said Felicity. Even I knew that was a mistake.

"That's kids' stuff," said Dave, pulling a face.

"No, she's got it wrong," said Kenny. "I think she likes… classical music."

He pulled an even worse face.

"It could be country and western," I said. His face lit up.

"That's right. It *was* country and western," said Kenny. "I remember now."

"At least she's got good taste in music," said Dave. We all nodded enthusiastically.

By now Dave was looking seriously interested, but the whistle had gone for lessons. We headed back to the classroom.

Felicity said, "I didn't know Brown Owl liked country and western."

Honestly, what is she like? She can be so dozy sometimes.

But we knew Dave was interested because after that he stopped mentioning Pamela Anderson every time he saw us and started asking how Madeline was. Felicity was so convinced we'd got it sorted that she started doing little drawings of what kind of bridesmaid's dresses we would all wear.

"Look, don't bank on it," I said. "We still haven't talked to Brown Owl."

That night it was Brownies. Our Brownie pack meets in the church hall on a Thursday night. It's not a very big pack but there are four sixes. Me and Kenny and Fliss are all sixers. Lyndz is my seconder and Rosie has joined Kenny's six. At the moment we're all working on our Brownie Highway. It's the last of our Brownie journeys. Some of us are nearly old enough to leave Brownies. We're writing a play and making puppets with Snowy Owl. We're supposed to be doing a puppet show for our mums and dads, but it's taken us weeks just to make the puppets.

We were all sitting round a table and Brown Owl came over to see how we were getting on. She sat down with us, so I grabbed the opportunity. I pretended to be dead laid back.

"Brown Owl, what kind of music d'you like?"

"All sorts," she said.

"But what's your favourite?"

She shrugged. "Jazz... opera..."

"Opera?" I said.

"Don't you like Oasis?" said Lyndz.

"I've never heard them," said Brown Owl. Lyndsey's jaw dropped.

"What about country and western?" said Kenny, desperately.

"Yes, it's OK. I like all sorts."

We let out a sigh of relief.

"Brown Owl, how old are you?" Felicity asked.

"Felicity!" said Snowy Owl, shocked.

"Never you mind," said Brown Owl, smiling. "It's not polite to ask a lady her age."

Fliss said, "Sorry."

"I should think so too," said Snowy Owl.

Why are grown-ups so funny about their

age? I don't get it. But at least it had made Brown Owl smile. Then Rosie went too far.

"Brown Owl, have you got a boyfriend?"

Brown Owl's face went all serious and stern-looking and she got up and walked off. "You just concentrate on your puppets," she told us, "instead of my love-life."

"What did you have to go and say that for?" I hissed at Rosie.

"How else are we going to find out?" she hissed back.

Snowy Owl looked at us suspiciously.

"We were only wondering," I said, trying to look innocent. "She just doesn't seem very happy."

Snowy looked over to make sure Brown Owl couldn't hear her.

"She hasn't got a boyfriend," she whispered. "And it's time she had. No one's worth getting yourself that miserable over. I've told her that, but she's not ready to hear it yet. So don't you lot go upsetting her any more, d'you hear?"

We all nodded and looked at one another, but we didn't say anything else to Snowy Owl. We just got on with painting our puppet heads. You can't tell with grown-ups who you can trust and who you can't. But at least one thing was clear, Brown Owl needed our help, even if she didn't know it yet.

CHAPTER SIX

We thought we'd at least got Dave on our side. So it was a bit of a surprise that on Friday, when we mentioned it, he burst out laughing.

"Are you still on about that?" he said. "Don't you think that joke's wearing a bit thin?"

"But it's not a joke," said Kenny.

"We're deadly serious," I said.

"Deadly?" said Dave. "That sounds pretty serious. Come on, guys, you're in my way." And then we had to move because he wanted to start polishing the hall floor.

Fliss had one last go. "What would we have to do to convince you?" she asked him.

"Get me a photo." A photo, I thought, where are we going to get that? "Or, better still, get her to send me a letter," he said, smiling.

A photo was bad enough, but a letter was completely out of the question. Or I thought it was, until on the way home from school, Lyndz had one of her crackpot ideas.

"*We* could write one," she said.

"We'd never get away with it," I said. "He'd know it was our writing."

I'm the only one who can do joined-up handwriting that doesn't look like a bowl of spaghetti. But nobody would believe it belonged to a grown-up who works in a bank.

"We don't need to *write* it," said Kenny.

"We can print it on the computer. And it's dead easy to fake a signature. I copy my dad's all the time."

"Oh, really?" I said, raising one eyebrow. I'm the only one who can do that trick, too.

Kenny grinned. "Just the odd cheque when my pocket money runs out."

"Honestly?" said Felicity, who'd believe anything you told her.

"She's joking," I said, tapping the side of my head. "Derrr!"

"It's just a game," said Kenny. "I've got this really ancient prescription pad my dad gave me. I sign them Doctor *McKenzie*. It looks dead cool."

"But what would we put in the letter?" I said. I still didn't like the idea.

"You are a handsome hunk. I lurv you," said Lyndz, rolling her eyes and then collapsing in a fit of giggles.

"We were born to be together." Kenny clutched her heart and puckered her lips.

After that the pair of them just went a bit haywire. Kenny started doing a terrible French accent and Lyndz kept fluttering her eyelashes.

"All right, calm down, you dodos," I said, but none of us could stop laughing. People were staring at us across the street. It was really wicked.

But I remember thinking of what my grandma says, when things get out of hand: "You mark my words, this'll all end in tears."

It was right in the middle of all this that we found out a bit more about Rosie's family. We often walk past her house on our way home from school and hope she'll invite us in, but so far no such luck. I know some people's parents are dead strict and don't like other kids in their house. Thank goodness mine aren't like that – but neither was her mum. She often said, "Rosie, don't keep your friends on the step. Ask them in." But she wouldn't and we couldn't work out why.

We knew her dad didn't live with them, she'd told us that, but then lots of people in our class haven't got a dad at home.

Fliss hasn't. She's got Andy, her mum's boyfriend, but he's not her dad. Her proper dad lives in the next street with his girlfriend Maria and the new baby, Posie. Fliss and her brother go round every Friday to her dad's for tea, but they don't live with him.

Also, Rosie had told us about her brother Adam. We hadn't seen him yet because he goes to a special school. We knew he used a wheelchair; we'd seen it in the back of her mum's car. But Rosie said he couldn't talk either, so we thought perhaps she didn't want us to go to her house because of Adam. But we were wrong about that too.

I had to go and put my foot in it, didn't I? Me and my big mouth!

We were leaning on Rosie's gate; I said, "It's Friday today, if we had a sleepover tonight we could write the letter and take it to Dave's tomorrow."

"Wicked!" said Fliss. "And we could make all our plans for OBD."

I kept staring at Rosie's house, hoping she would take the hint, but she didn't.

"Well, we can't have it at mine," said Fliss. "My mum still hasn't got over the bubble-bath episode." Some time I'll tell you that story!

"Don't look at me," said Lyndz. "My mum and dad are decorating, *again!*" Lyndz's mum and dad are always doing something to her house. Extending it or decorating it or taking it apart and putting it back together again.

"I suppose I could ask mine," Kenny offered. "But Monster-features will only interfere." Kenny has the worst sister the human imagination could conjure up. We call her *Molly the Monster*. And poor old

Kenny has to share a bedroom with her!

We'd already had the one last week at mine, so that left just one person and I was getting tired of dropping hints.

"What about at yours?" I said to Rosie, straight out, just like that. But the minute I'd said it, I wished I hadn't. Rosie went bright red and shook her head.

"Why not?" I said.

"Because," said Rosie, starting to look as if she might cry.

"Look, if it's because of Adam..." I started, without knowing how I was going to finish.

"We don't mind, honest," said Fliss.

"No," said Lyndz. "I've got an uncle in a wheelchair."

"So?" said Rosie. "What about it? This is nothing to do with Adam, you stupids. It's the state my house is in." And then she burst into tears.

She told us her dad was a builder. He'd bought the house to do up, but he'd met his girlfriend soon after they'd moved in. Now he'd gone off and left them in this amazing big house which Rosie said was a complete tip.

"He says he'll fix it, but he never does. It's horrible! There's hardly any carpets. My bedroom's got no paper on the walls."

"We don't care about wallpaper," I said, trying to make her feel better.

"Well, I do," she said, going through her gate and slamming it behind her. "It's not fair. I hate everybody!" And she went up her path, sobbing.

All the others were looking at me as if to say, "Well, I hope you're satisfied now."

But I wasn't. I felt terrible. I hadn't meant to make her cry. I went straight home and asked my mum if we could *please* have another sleepover at my house. I even got down on my knees into my famous begging pose.

"Pretty please," I said, "with cherries on the top."

My mum looked down at me pretending to be a well-trained dog, and shook her head. "I don't know what makes you think that performance is likely to persuade anyone," she said.

But it did. I got straight on the phone and rang round.

"It's on for tonight! Sleepover, at mine. Seven o'clock."

"You're wonderful," I told my mum. "I'm your slave for ever. Whatever you desire, command and I will obey."

My mum just grinned and kept on watching the news, but my dad said, "Right, that's two cups of tea now and extra washing-up for a week."

"It's a deal," I said. "You're the best." Thank goodness for groovy parents!

CHAPTER SEVEN

I think they started to get suspicious that night when we were so keen to go to bed early. Usually I have to beg and plead with them to stay up late on a Friday for *Friends*. It's my best programme! Coo-el. But there we go. Sometimes there are more important things even than *Friends*! So by eight o'clock we were all in our jimjams in my bedroom, talking really quietly.

Kenny and I were sharing a bed again, Lyndz and Felicity had got the bunks and Rosie was on the camp bed this time. She was looking like a wet weekend again, even though nobody had mentioned her outburst at the gate. It felt funny, because we were all thinking about it, even though we weren't saying anything, if you see what I mean. It was as though there was an elephant standing in the corner but no one was mentioning the fact.

"Right, let's get started," said old bossy-boots Fliss. "Who's doing the typing?"

I can tell you now what she'll be when she grows up: a teacher! She's always practising bossing us about.

"I'll do it," I said, turning my computer on. The others all crowded round me. "Right, I'm ready," I said.

Then we all sat there looking at the blank screen.

"Dear Dave…" said Felicity. Then she sat there looking very pleased with herself.

"Oh, good start," I said. "Well, that's the

hard bit over."

"'I really fancy you,'" said Kenny. "'How about going out with me?'"

"That is so sad," I said.

Rosie shook her head. "Brown Owl definitely wouldn't say that."

"So what would she say, clever clogs?" said Kenny.

"Something like: 'I've seen you around school; you look like a nice person.'"

"You look like a *nice person*," said Kenny in a whiny voice. "That's so naff. Where's the romance in that?"

"There's no *lurv* in that," agreed Lyndsey, getting all giggly. I could just see them starting each other off again.

"Listen! Listen," I said. "Rosie's right. It doesn't have to be sloppy stuff. I'll write down what she just said."

"Then say something about how she likes country and western music," said Rosie.

"Oh, yes," said Fliss. "That's important,

Frankie. Don't forget that bit."

"Yeah, yeah. I've put that. Then what?"

"Put: 'I'd like to go out with you. How about it?'" said Kenny.

I wrote: *'I'd like to go out with you.'* Brown Owl wouldn't say "how about it"!

"Anything else?"

"That's enough, isn't it?" said Rosie.

"Don't we want to say where they could meet?"

"The bus station."

"Outside the chippie."

"The park gates."

"Put: 'I'll be wearing a red carnation',"
said Kenny.

It was like a story we were making up. We could have put anything. Dave might turn up, but there was one bit we still hadn't worked out.

"How on earth are we going to get Brown Owl there?"

"We'll just choose a place where we know Brown Owl's going to be," said

Kenny, as if that was the easiest thing in the world.

"Not at Brownies. She won't want him turning up there," said Fliss.

"Or in the bank," I said.

"Or at her house, I guess," said Lyndz.

"Where else does she go?" asked Rosie.

"She shops on a Saturday at the SavaCentre. I always see her when I go with my mum," said Felicity.

"Oh, how *romantic*!" said Kenny.

"Meet me by the frozen peas," said Lyndz.

"We can cuddle by the cabbages," said Kenny. They can be so silly.

"D'you think she'll be there tomorrow?" said Rosie, ignoring them.

"Probs," said Felicity.

"Tomorrow's no good, I've got badminton," said Kenny.

"Not in the afternoon, you haven't," I said.

"D'you think you could get your mum

and dad to take us?" said Fliss.

"All of us?"

"Yes. We all need to be there."

"Tell them it's for a project we're doing at school," said Kenny.

Well, that was almost true, wasn't it? I just wouldn't tell them the project was called Operation Blind Date. And it *was* in a good cause.

I finished the letter off: *I'll be shopping in the SavaCentre on Saturday afternoon. I'll see you there.*

"How shall I sign it?"

"'Lots of love and kisses,'" said Kenny, getting really stupid.

"'Yours affectionately, Madeline,'" suggested Fliss.

But none of us could spell "affectionately" so we just put: *Love from...* Then I printed it off and Kenny signed it with a huge scribble.

"What's that supposed to say?"

"Madeline."

"You can't read it."

"You're not supposed to be able to read it," said Kenny. "That's what signatures are like."

"He can read the letter, that's the important thing," Lyndz agreed.

"When are we going to give it to him?" said Rosie.

"We'll have to take it round in the morning," I said.

"I can't," said Kenny. "Badminton."

"I've got to look after Spike," said Lyndz. That's her baby brother. "But I can come back after dinner."

"OK," I said. "That means *we'll* have to take it," I told Fliss and Rosie. "We can take Pepsi for a walk past his house."

By now, my mum was coming in to see if we wanted drinks and biscuits. I knew we'd been far too quiet and she was looking suspicious. So we had our usual silly half-hour before we got into bed. You know the kind of thing: three rounds of International Gladiators, which as usual ended up with Lyndz having one of her fits of hiccups.

"OK. Lights out," said Dad. "Nighty-night. Don't let the werewolves bite."

"It's bedbugs," said Felicity, giggling.

"Not in this h-o-u-s-e," my dad howled. Sometimes parents can be so embarrassing!

After he'd gone down and we were lying in the dark, Rosie said, "Thanks for inviting me again, even though I told you I couldn't have you round at my house."

"It's OK," said Lyndsey. "We don't mind, do we?"

"No," said the others. "It's not your fault."

In a way I didn't mind either. Rosie was sort of growing on me. She had some good ideas and she could be quite a laugh, but there was a principle here.

My mum and dad are both lawyers and

they're always telling me about principles. If you agree to something, you should stick to it. Like if I say, OK, I'll set the table every night or wash up on Mondays and Wednesdays, then I should do it. Or if I don't like my dad interrupting me when I'm watching *Home and Away*, I shouldn't barge in on him when he's watching the news. So if we want to be in a Sleepover Club and sleep at other people's houses, then it's only right that we let everyone sleep at our house. That's fair, isn't it?

So I said, "But I still don't see why we can't sleep at yours, if your mum'll let us."

"Oh, Frankie," the others started up. "She's already told us why."

"Just because her bedroom's in a tip? She's not seen Kenny's yet."

"Thanks a bunch," said Kenny.

I said, "You know what I mean." Kenny's famous for how untidy she is. It drives her sister barmy.

"Well, it wouldn't bother me whether there was paper on the walls," Kenny agreed.

"Nor me," said Lyndsey, "as long as we have a laugh."

At first Rosie still didn't say anything, but after a bit she said, "Well, OK, if you're sure. I'll see what my mum says."

I thought, two-one, yeah! But I didn't say anything and neither did anyone else. In fact, the silence got a bit creepy, so we were all relieved when Fliss said, "Isn't it time for our midnight feast?"

"Yeah," I said. "Let's see what we've got tonight. Oh, brillo, rhubarb and apple fizzers!"

CHAPTER EIGHT

Next morning, as soon as I woke up, I went into mum and dad's room. They were already awake, sitting up in bed, as usual on a Saturday, reading the papers.

"Anyone like a cuppa?"

"We've got one, thanks," said Dad. "Pity you weren't up ten minutes earlier."

"But you can let Pepsi out," said Mum.

"No problem," I said. "I'll take her for a nice long walk later. Anything else? Breakfast in bed? Bowl of cereal? Piece of toast? Bacon butty?"

I think I must have been overdoing it,

because they both looked at me over the top of their glasses.

"What are you after?" said Mum.

"Nothing," I said, as if butter wouldn't melt in my mouth. "Just trying to be helpful."

"Francesca? What's going on?"

"What are you after?"

"I was just wondering if you'd like to take us with you to the supermarket."

"All five of you?" said Mum.

"Why would I?" said Dad.

"It would save time. We could help you."

"I think not," said Dad. "I suspect it would take me five times as long."

"Oh, please, Dad. It's really important. It's for a project for school. We need some information on... prices."

"Well, that's different," said Dad.

"Why didn't you say that in the first place?" said Mum. "It's always the best policy to start with the truth. You're much more likely to get what you want that way."

Well, that made me feel really lousy. I hate fibbing to my parents. It always makes me feel horrible. My mum's right: if I ask for something straight out, they usually say yes. But this time was different. I just knew, if I told them the whole story, they wouldn't understand. So what else could I do?

When I got back in my bedroom, I should have guessed it was too quiet to be true. The others suddenly all yanked back their covers and hurled their pillows at me.

"Pack it in!" I yelled. "That's the last time I do you lot a favour." I was sitting on the floor, surrounded by pillows.

"What did they say?" asked Kenny.

"They said yes, of course," I said.

"Wicked!"

"One-nil," said Kenny.

"Frankie's the greatest," said Lyndz.

"Humph," I said, grumpily. And I didn't cheer up until they'd all grovelled at my feet and called me a star. "That's more like it," I said.

After breakfast Kenny's mum came and collected her to take her to badminton and she took Lyndsey home at the same time.

"Is it all right if they come back this afternoon," I said, "to go to the supermarket?"

"We're doing this shopping project at school and we've got to collect some information," said Kenny.

"Comparing prices," said Fliss.

"Which are the cheapest brands," said Lyndz.

Suddenly this little white lie had turned into a complete story. I was almost beginning to believe it myself.

Fliss and Rosie and I walked Pepsi along

the road I usually take to school. The letter was burning a hole in my pocket. I couldn't wait to get rid of it. I was feeling pretty nervous, but I didn't say anything because by now Fliss was really starting to panic. She kept stopping in the middle of the pavement and gasping.

"What if he isn't in?" she said.

"We'll post it through the letterbox," said Rosie.

"That's what you do with letters," I reminded her.

We walked on a bit further, then she stopped again.

"But then how will we know he's got it? What if he doesn't open it before this afternoon? What if he's out? What if he's ill? What if he's gone on holiday?"

"What if he's been abducted by aliens?" I suggested.

"What if he's turned overnight into a dog?" said Rosie.

"A dog?" said Fliss, frowning.

"Joke," I said. "It was a joke."

"Well, I don't think it was very funny," said Fliss.

But me and Rosie did. We really cracked up.

When we got close to Dave's house, we all completely lost our nerve. I wasn't absolutely sure I knew which house was his. It's a road where all the houses look the same. Fliss insisted it was number 37, the one with a green front door, but I had a feeling it was the one two doors down with a black front door.

We stood across the road hoping he'd come out or appear at the window. But he didn't. After five minutes, by which time I was convinced everyone in the road was watching us behind their curtains, or, worse still, phoning the police, I suddenly remembered something.

"Dave doesn't have a car," I said. There was a car in the drive of number 37.

"It could be a visitor's," Fliss pointed

out. She hates to lose an argument.

So Rosie said, "Why don't we just knock on the door and ask?"

"I'm not," said Fliss.

"I'd better not. I've got the dog," I said. "She might growl at him." The other two looked at me. Pepsi hardly ever growls. She's the softest dog on four legs.

"Oh, I'll go," said Rosie. Just like that. She held her hand out for the letter and then marched straight over. She knocked on the door and waited. She looked over her shoulder and smiled. We waved to her. We were seriously impressed.

But nothing happened. So she knocked again, and waited what seemed like ages. This time when she looked back at us she wasn't smiling. Then she must have heard someone coming because she just dropped the letter on the step and ran. So we ran as well, right down the road, as if Dracula had come to the door.

But when we'd got far enough away, I

stopped and let myself look back. Dave was standing at the door in his pyjamas, shaking his head and grinning. So I waved to him, then I ran to catch up with the others. Now at least we knew he'd got it.

CHAPTER NINE

On the way to the supermarket, I sat by Dad in the front seat and the others piled into the back of the estate. Dad looked over his shoulder.

"You don't seem to have much with you. Don't you need little clipboards or something?"

"It's all right," I said, waving my notebook. "I'll write it all down. They can copy off me on Monday."

"Very public-spirited," said Dad.

When we got into the store, Dad told us. "Now, no one is to set foot outside the store without me. It's quite busy, so try not to get in anyone's way. Meet me at the checkouts in one hour. Who's got a watch?"

We all put up our hands, just as if we were at school.

"OK," I said. "Synchronise watches."

Dad said, "I make it 2.05 precisely."

Lyndz stared at her watch. "Does that mean the long hand's before or after the two?"

"After!" said Kenny.

"Honestly, Lyndz," I said. "Are you ever going to learn to tell the time?"

"It's not my fault. It's this watch."

She certainly would have got on better if she'd had a digital like the rest of us, but Lyndz has a real mental block about telling the time anyway. She always says, "Why does it matter?"

Dad laughed and went off. "Remember, no mischief! I don't want to have to pay for any breakages. Do you understand?"

We all nodded and smiled. Yes, yes, we understood. Famous last words.

We decided to split up and take an aisle each, to see if there was any sign of Brown Owl or Dave. I got Pet Foods and Toiletries. I couldn't believe how many people there were shopping that afternoon, and most of them seemed to be buying dog biscuits and shampoo. We kept waving to each other and shaking our heads, then going back up the aisle we'd come down, in case we'd missed them.

After about a quarter of an hour I tried to round the others up, but every time I got to the bottom of an aisle I'd see them disappearing back up it. I was nearly tearing my hair out. Now I knew what it was like being a mum in charge of four naughty kids.

"Right, let's try and stay together," I said.

"Yes, Mum," said Kenny, grinning.

We saw plenty of other people from school or Brownies with their mums, but no Brown Owl. In fact, we bumped into Felicity's Auntie Jill. You know, Snowy Owl.

"What are you doing here?" she asked Fliss.

"Helping Frankie's dad," she said, looking a bit guilty.

"He must be doing a big shop to need five helpers."

"Have you seen Brown Owl anywhere?" I asked.

"She was parking her car in the car park as I drove in. Why?"

"No reason," said Fliss.

"We've got a message for her, that's all," said Rosie.

"From my mum," I added hurriedly.

"Well, she'll be in here somewhere. Now, don't get into any trouble," she warned Fliss. "You do exactly what Mr

Thomas tells you."

While we'd been talking to Snowy Owl, Kenny and Lyndsey had wandered off.

"Where have they gone?" I asked Rosie.

"Search me," she said.

"Well, let's try and find them. Then we've got to stay together."

Brown Owl was obviously around and it was just a matter of time before we found her. We hadn't seen Dave yet. We just had to hope he'd turn up. But we couldn't find Kenny and Lyndz anywhere and I was getting really worried.

What I didn't say, but I was certainly thinking, was that sometimes, when those two get together, they go completely haywire. I just hoped this wasn't one of those times. But, then, as we stood at one end of the Wine and Beer aisle, I saw something at the other end that told me it *was* one of those times.

Lyndz was racing round with a full

supermarket trolley, which would have been bad enough. What made it worse was that it was full of Kenny.

We set off as fast as we could to follow them. But we'd hardly gone a few steps when we stopped dead. Coming down the aisle towards us was Dave.

He looked really different. We'd never seen him except in his overalls or work clothes. He looked even nicer than he did at school. He did look really dishy. He'd got a leather jacket on and jeans and black leather boots. He was carrying a basket but all he'd got in it so far were a couple of tins.

We stood there, sort of hidden by a family with a full shopping trolley, not sure whether to rush up and say hello or go back the way we'd come. Behind him, just coming round the corner, we spotted Brown Owl. That made our minds up for us. Fortunately neither of them had seen us yet.

"Quick," I said. "This way." And I led Fliss and Rosie backwards up the aisle.

"Wasn't that Dave?" Fliss almost squealed, craning her neck to see him. I grabbed her by the arm and pulled her back.

"Yes," I said through gritted teeth. "Now, tell me something I don't know."

"Wasn't that Brown Owl as well?" said Rosie.

"Yes, it was, but more important right now, where are Kenny and Lyndz?"

Suddenly we heard a noise from the next aisle which sort of answered the question.

It wasn't exactly a crash. It would have been, if they'd been glass bottles. But this sounded more like skittles being knocked over. About two hundred of them. It was a whole display of plastic bottles of mineral water. They landed with a dull thud and then rolled in all directions.

A Boyfriend for Brown Owl

I knew straight away who'd run into them. You didn't have to be Mastermind to work that out. This was a big store. I just hoped my dad was right at the other end of it.

CHAPTER TEN

As we turned the corner, there were people picking up bottles in every direction. Kenny and Lyndz, with faces the colour of bottled beetroot, were in the middle, trying to put the display back together again. One or two of the bottles had exploded and there was a fizzy river running down the aisle. A worried-looking boy came with a mop.

My brain felt as if it was about to explode too. I was thinking about Dave and Brown Owl in the next aisle and wondering whether they'd suddenly appear and walk straight into it all. Even worse, I was dreading my dad coming round the corner and finding us.

Fliss and Rosie and I rushed over to help collect up the bottles, but by now the manager had arrived. That's put the king in the cake, I thought, now we're going to get it. But all he was bothered about was getting the mess cleared up. He didn't seem to care how it had happened. He took the bottles off us and sort of shooed us away. So we all ran off before he changed his mind.

"You pair are too lucky to live," I said.

"It wasn't our fault, was it?" Kenny said to Lyndz. "It was an accident." But then they gave themselves away by giggling.

"Come on," I said. "They're over here." I pointed down the next aisle. And there they were – gone.

"This way," I said, "follow me! And stick together."

At the end of each aisle we peered

round the corner shelves until we found them.

Brown Owl was reading the ingredients on a jar of pasta sauce. Dave was having a conversation with a five-year-old I recognised from school and his mum and grandma. But then he turned our way and walked towards us... and towards Brown Owl.

"Quick!" I said. And we all squeezed behind a stack of baked beans. "Anybody knock these over," I warned them, "and you're dead."

Dave had stopped beside Brown Owl and was waiting for her to move so that he could reach a jar of pasta sauce for himself.

"Don't they make a nice couple?" whispered Fliss.

"They like the same pasta sauce," whispered Rosie.

"Ahhh, that's nice," said Lyndz.

"So a-romantic!" said Kenny in a stupid

Italian accent.

"Shhh!" I said, terrified they'd hear and look over and see us watching them.

Brown Owl suddenly realised she was in Dave's way and smiled at him and moved along until she was out of his way and then stopped to check her list. She'd got a full trolley and she was crossing a lot off. It looked as if she was just about finished. This could be our last chance.

"What are we going to do?" said Fliss.

"I don't know," I said.

Dave was coming straight towards us. So Kenny and I popped up and waved to him, then we both pointed at Brown Owl.

Dave stopped and frowned, but we kept on pointing until he turned and looked back over his shoulder. When he saw Brown Owl, he looked at us with his head on one side and then he pointed at her as well. We all popped up and nodded.

Dave smiled and headed back towards her. We weren't close enough to hear what he said but we'd all got our fingers and toes crossed. I don't know about the others but I was too nervous to breathe.

Brown Owl was looking very surprised. Dave looked as if he was telling her a joke, but she didn't seem to be getting it. She just kept on frowning until suddenly the penny seemed to drop. Dave nodded in our direction and Brown Owl looked over too.

We all ducked down but I think she saw us. Then she started to shake her head as if she couldn't believe what he was telling her. They'd *been* talking quietly, but we heard the next thing loud and clear.

"I'm *not* looking for a boyfriend. What letter? I didn't write any letter."

And then the worst thing of all happened. Dave took out the letter and showed it to her. When Brown Owl read it, she sort of erupted and went into orbit.

We didn't wait around to find out what happened next, because I suddenly remembered my dad and realised what time it was.

"It's gone quarter past three," I shrieked. "Come on!" I raced off, with the others dodging shopping trolleys behind me. When we reached the checkout, Dad was standing there with his mad-as-a-hatter face on.

I raised my hands. "Dad, we're really, truly, genuinely, totally, completely sorry."

"We got lost," said Kenny.

"Carried away," said Fliss.

"Forgot the time," said Lyndz.

"Just spare me the excuses," said Dad, already halfway out of the door.

We raced after him, hardly daring to look back in case Brown Owl was following us. We helped Dad lift the shopping into the back of the car in record time. Then we jumped in the car and kept our heads down. Nobody spoke all the way home and on the way back

Dad dropped the others off.

Kenny was last to be dropped off. As we drove away, she gave me a good-luck sign. I had a feeling I was going to need it – and I was right, wasn't I?

GOODBYE

So now you know the whole story. We had no idea it would turn out like this. We were just trying to be helpful. Grounded, my mum said. And it wasn't even my fault. Well, there we go. Like my grandma says, life's very unfair.

I wish I was a fly on the wall in our lounge right now. I'd love to hear Brown Owl's side of the story. But then again, perhaps I wouldn't.

It seems a real shame; she and Dishy Dave made such a nice couple.

Uh-oh. What was that? I think it was the front door closing. Quick, let's look out the window, but don't let her see you, whatever you do. That's Brown Owl all right. Thank goodness she's gone. If she's told them everything, I'm not worth a life.

"Francesca! Please come down here, *this minute.*"

Uh-oh. This could be the end. The end of the Sleepover Club. Possibly the end of Francesca Theresa Thomas. Well, say a prayer for me.

Goodbye. Farewell. Au revoir (that's French, in case you don't know). Arrivederci (that's Italian).

I bet you're impressed. I can say hello and goodbye in five different languages. My grandad taught me the last time I went to stay. Now, what was it in Spanish...?

"Francesca! I mean *now!*"

"Coming, Mum!"

I'd better go. Keep your fingers crossed for me. See ya!

Theres a Lot
of things Suer

The Sleepover Club at Lyndsey's

TOO SCARED TO SLEEP

Theres a lot of things a super
star can do! yee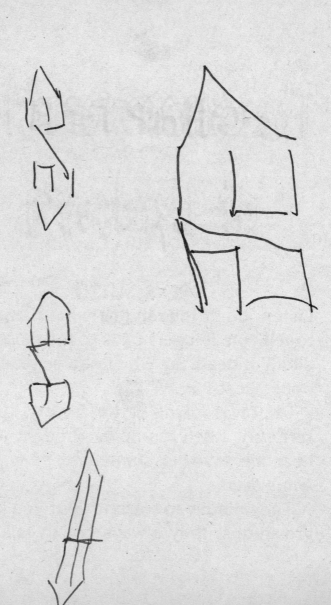

o

CHAPTER ONE

Listen, don't tell anyone what I'm going to tell you. If it gets back to my mum and dad, I'm dead. So, when you've read this book... eat it.

OK, I was joking! But seriously, I mean *seriously*, I bet you never thought you'd hear me say this: *sometimes parents do know best!*

They did try to warn us. But you know grown-ups: they always try to talk you out of anything exciting you want to do. So, of course, we took no notice. And I suppose we were a bit OTT, because it was the first time we'd been allowed to sleep over since all the trouble with Brown Owl.

But *this* story is about Lyndsey's birthday party and what happened when we all slept over at her house and watched a scary video. We'd have been fine if Kenny hadn't started us off telling horror stories and then talking to ghosts. After that we were all too scared to sleep. So we were still awake in the middle of the night, when the bedroom door creaked open and *someone* came into the room...

But before I get started I suppose I'd better tell you who everyone is. I've got a photo of us somewhere. Ta-daaa! The Sleepover Club.

That's me on the end: Francesca Thomas, but you can call me Frankie.

On the other end – in the baseball cap – is my best friend Laura McKenzie. She's the wild one; we call her Kenny.

That's Fliss at the top – Felicity Sidebotham, or, as the boys at school call her, Flossy *Slidebottom*.

Lyndsey Collins is in the middle of everyone. You remember her, she's the hiccup queen. We call her Lyndz.

And the last one's Rosie Cartwright. Rosie's just moved in round here. We don't really know her very well yet, but she seems OK, so far.

So that's all of us.

Mostly we sleep over at each other's houses at weekends or in the holidays. But best of all are special times like

Bonfire Night or Hallowe'en. Or birthdays!

I've got to wait ages for mine; it's not until April. I'm Aries. My horoscope book says I'm a born leader – bold, brave, decisive and quick-witted. Yeah, that's me!

I'm really into horoscopes. My dad says they're a load of rubbish but then he's Taurus – the Bull! He's dead stubborn.

Fliss has already had her birthday. She's Virgo, which means she's a bit of a fussy. Fliss likes everything just so! Her birthday sleepover was another adventure, but we won't go into that now.

Kenny and Rosie have to wait even longer for their birthdays. Kenny's Gemini, a real split personality, and Rosie's a crab. That just describes her – prickly on the outside and soft inside. But Lyndz is Libra, dead soft-hearted. Lyndz is the one who always makes the peace and tries to look after everyone. It was because she felt sorry for Rosie that we let her join the Sleepover Club in the first place.

Even when it came to her own birthday party, Lyndz was so busy trying to keep everyone happy she couldn't decide what *she* wanted to do. I thought we'd never get it sorted out. You can probably guess who was playing up, as usual – Fusspot Fliss.

CHAPTER TWO

OK, let me tell you how it all started. One day after school we were at netball practice. Well, we weren't doing much practising. We were waiting for Miss Burnie to find the key to the PE store. She's always losing things. We all like her but, boy, is she dozy! We usually spend the first ten minutes of practice time looking for the key, or her whistle, or her plimmies. Or her! Quite often we find her having a cup of tea in the staff room – she's forgotten it's Tuesday and we're outside, standing round, shivering. So this day we were leaning against the PE store, waiting for her.

We're all in the netball team now. I play Goal Shooter and, even if I say so myself, I'm an ace shooter. Kenny's Goal Attack and together we're a pretty dynamic duo. Lyndz is Goal Defence and Fliss is Centre. But now Rosie's come and she plays Centre too. So that spells t-r-o-u-b-l-e.

At the moment she's in the second team but Miss Burnie's promised to try her out for the first team soon. Fliss isn't happy about it, I can tell you.

I said to Fliss, "Why don't you swap with Rosie and play Wing Attack?" But you know Fliss. She looked at me as if I'd suggested she cut her arm off.

"Why don't *you* swap with Rosie, if you think it's such a good idea?" she said.

"Because Rosie isn't a shooter," I said.

Rosie sort of looked down and said, "Don't worry. I don't care anyway." Which is a big fat porky-pie. You can see she wants to be in the first team like the rest of us, but she wouldn't admit it even if we put her in a bath of snails.

"Listen," I said, "if Rosie was in the first team, we could get rid of Alana Banana."

"Yeah. Four-one!" said Kenny, who can't stand her.

She's not really called that. Her name's Alana Palmer. She is too boring to live. She sometimes hangs around with the M&Ms. The M&Ms are two girls in our class: Emma Hughes and Emily Berryman. They are *so* stuck-up. They're teacher's pets and Brown Owl's pets and everybody-in-the-world's pets and we can't stand them, but fortunately the M&Ms can't play netball.

"I don't see why *I* should swap," said Fliss.

We were definitely heading for one of our arguments. So Lyndz, the peacemaker, changed the subject.

"I can't decide what to do for my birthday and it's only two weeks away."

"Surely we'll have a sleepover?" said Kenny.

"Yeah, but we've got to do something else as well," said Lyndz.

"Let's go skating," I said.

"Let's have a video," said Kenny.

"We could have *Babe*," said Fliss. "It's so sweet."

I said, "We've all seen that."

"Let's get a horror video," said Kenny. "One of the Freddy films."

"Yeah! They're great," said Rosie.

"How do you know?" I said.

"I've seen them."

"I bet you haven't," said Lyndz.

We knew Rosie was telling whoppers. It turned out she'd only seen the credits before her mum sent her to bed.

"Anyway," said Fliss, "you all know I

don't like horror films."

"Look, this is Lyndsey's birthday," I said. "It's up to her to choose what she wants."

"Well, if she does choose a horror film, I won't be able to come, and I don't think that's very fair, do you?"

Fliss is always talking about what's fair and making us vote on things. But sometimes it doesn't matter whether it's fair or not. It's like my gran says, you can't please everyone. I think when it's your birthday you should please yourself. That's what I'd have done.

But Lyndz is different. "I don't mind what we get."

"*Babe*," said Fliss again.

"We've *seen* it," I said, through gritted teeth.

Lyndz shrugged. "I don't mind."

Well, I minded and I was about to say so when Miss Burnie turned up with the key. So then netball practice started and there was no more time to talk.

But later I phoned Kenny to tell her what I thought about it. I always ring Kenny if I want a moan. Sometimes we talk for hours. But sometimes, if she's in one of those on-another-planet moods, I might as well save my breath to cool my porridge, as my gran says. This was one of *those* times.

I could tell she wasn't listening because I could hear the TV channels in the background. I could just see her sitting on the sofa with the mobile phone in one hand and the remote in the other, channel-hopping. She does it all the time. It drives her mum and dad barmy. And me. So I made her turn the sound down at least.

"*Listen*," I said. "Fliss is always going on about things not being fair. But this is Lyndz's birthday. If she wants to see a horror film and the rest of us want to see a horror film, we should see a horror film, shouldn't we? But we're not, are we? We're going to see *Babe*, which we've all seen already. And why are we seeing it again? Because Fliss wants to see it again, that's why. Now you tell me, where's the fairness in that?"

"Search me. Gotta go, Frankie, *Rugrats* is on."

"Oh, thanks for nothing. I'll ring you again."

"OK. Bye."

See what I mean? Waste of time, or what? So then I rang Lyndsey.

"Hi, it's Frankie."

"Hi."

"I've been thinking about your birthday."

"Oh, yeah?"

"I was thinking, if you really want a horror film…"

"I don't mind."

"Don't keep saying that. It's your birthday, you should choose."

"I'd have to ask my mum and dad."

"Just think about it, that's all."

"OK."

I didn't really expect her to take any notice, so I was pretty surprised after tea when Lyndz rang me back, dead excited.

"Frankie, is that you? I've asked my mum and dad. Do you want the good news?"

"Yes. Go on."

"They didn't say no."

"That's supposed to be good news? But did they say yes?"

"No... but they didn't say no. Don't worry, I'll work on them."

CHAPTER THREE

And she must have done, because a few days later they said, "Maybe. We'll see. As long as it's suitable for children."

"Oh, great big hairy deal," said Kenny. "If they're anything like my mum and dad, they think *Tom and Jerry* ought to have a 15 certificate."

The trouble was we'd watched everything PG that was worth watching already.

"I think they might let us see *Gremlins*," said Lyndz.

"Wicked!" said Rosie. "I saw that when Tiff and her boyfriend got it out."

Tiff is Rosie's older sister, she's fifteen. Perhaps Rosie had seen it, but we were getting used to her stories. We gave her our zip-fastener look. Up and down, dead fast.

"OK," she said, looking a bit sheepish, "I saw the first bit. They're dead-cute little furry things; really adorable. This man brings one home as a Christmas present for his son, but he forgets the rules and it gets wet and it makes lots more gremlins. Then he forgets the other rule and feeds them after midnight and that's when they turn nasty. *Then* I got sent to bed. Tiff said they were jumping out on people and getting them by the throat. One gets shut in the microwave and explodes all over the door."

"Oh, thanks, Rosie," I said. "Now we

don't need to bother seeing the film."

"Sounds brilliant," said Kenny.

"Sounds *gruesome*," said Fliss.

"I don't want anything *too* scary," said Lyndz. "Just scary enough."

I agreed with Lyndz. I didn't want anything *too* scary. When I'm with my friends I love getting that shivery feeling, like when you go to Alton Towers and your stomach seems to have gone for a walk somewhere and there's this empty space where it used to be and you all scream and scream **really loud**. That is coo-el. It's the best.

But sometimes, when I'm on my own, if I see something horrible on TV or read something scary in a book, it sort of sticks in the back of my mind. When I go to bed, the minute I turn out the light, it pops up and then I can't stop thinking about it. I lie there and I know it isn't real. But it *feels* real as if it's in the room with me. So I have to go downstairs and pretend I need a drink or I'm feeling a bit sick or something so my mum'll give me a cuddle.

I don't tell her the real reason I need a cuddle. No way. I know what she'd say: "I've *told* you not to watch programmes like that. You know they give you nightmares." *Or*, "Well, what do you expect, reading Bonechillers and Night-mares? At your age!"

But until you've seen something or read about it, how can you know if it's going to scare you? You can't, can you?

If I try to tell her I read scary stories because I like them, she looks at me as if I'm seriously weird. Just-scary-enough is brilliant. It's the best. But too scary is... *too scary*! You know what I mean.

The worst thing for me is *blood*. Kenny and me are total opposites. I'm really squeamish. So's my mum. It just makes us want to faint, or throw up. I don't mind reading about it, but I hate seeing it. It's gross.

But, listen, I don't want you telling the others about this. They think I'm the cool one. And most of the time I am. So keep it to yourself, all right?

Anyway, in the end Lyndz said she'd check it out with her brother Tom. He's really into horror. "I'll see what he thinks."

"Well, tell him we want something really gory with lots of blood in it," said Kenny.

Honestly, sometimes I think she must have been a vampire in another life.

Fliss was starting to look sick just talking about it. Fliss is worse than me. Much worse. She nearly passes out if she gets a splinter. And she's always having nightmares. She's the only person I know who screamed to come out of the cartoon of *Winnie-the-Pooh*. You know the bit where he gets stuck in Rabbit's hole and then comes out with a big POP! She *was* only three at the time, but she hasn't got much better.

But we were all starting to feel really bad about Fliss being left out and everything.

"Listen," I said, "just because you don't want to watch the film doesn't mean you can't come to the sleepover."

"No, of course not," said Lyndz.

"And what am I going to do while you're all watching it?" she snapped.

"We'll think of something," said Kenny.

But it wasn't Kenny's idea that she should sit in the corner with a woolly hat pulled over her eyes, which is what she did do. She came up with that idea all by herself. But then that's Fliss, nutty as a fruit cake, as my gran says.

CHAPTER FOUR

I'll tell you a bit about Lyndsey and her funny family next. When I say funny I mean funny-nice, not funny-horrid. They're really friendly and a great laugh, but they are a bit weird. And even more weird is Lyndsey's house.

Her dad's an art and design teacher and he's always redesigning their house, adding rooms or moving the stairs or the doors. One time when I went round I couldn't find the doorbell. The doorway was bricked up and the front door was round the side. Lyndz says sometimes even she can't find her way in.

At the moment her dad's building a new bedroom in the roof. Her baby brother needs a room of his own now, so he's going to have Lyndz's and she's having a new one, which will be great – more room for us when we sleep over. Her bedroom's so small the only way we can all get in is to take the bed out and lay our sleeping bags side by side on the floor as if we're laying Sardines. It's good fun, though.

Lyndz's mum used to teach art as well but now she teaches women how to have babies. She knows a lot about it; she's had five herself. Apart from Lyndz, they're all boys. That's why she likes it when *we* sleep over. She says it makes a nice change having a house full of girls after all those smelly boys!

Stuart's the oldest, he's sixteen. He's

mad about farming and he wants to go to agricultural college. But he's re-sitting his exams at the moment.

Tom's fourteen and he's *gorgeous*. Well, we used to think he was, before the sleepover! Lyndz says there're always girls from his class hanging around outside or ringing him up. He's into computer graphics and horror.

Lyndsey's in the middle. A rose between four thorns, her dad says.

Ben's four and a real little toughy. He's always jumping on you from behind and wanting to wrestle.

And then there's the baby, Sammy, but they call him Spike, because he's got this little tuft of hair which sticks up. He's six months old and just starting to crawl. You have to watch him like a hawk. He's always getting into places he shouldn't, which isn't difficult in that house.

Because she's got such a big family and all that building going on, Lyndz's mum's too busy to fuss about things like what time you go to bed or whether you've had a proper wash or how many biscuits you're allowed, you know the kind of thing. So sleepovers at Lyndz's are always great fun.

One of the best things about staying at Lyndz's is the fave set of dressing-up clothes she's got. Her mum had some of them when *she* was little. There are long dresses and cloaks and hats and belts and shoes and bags. Everything. We have mega dressing-up sessions and fashion shows. We use the back stairs to the attic as a catwalk, with Oasis playing really loud, pretending we're super-models.

That's another good thing about Lyndz's house – we can make a noise. Her mum's used to it, they're a pretty noisy family and Lyndz is the noisiest. We call her Slush Bucket, she's so noisy when she drinks. She giggles really loud too and when she gets hiccups you can nearly hear her in the next street.

But on the night of her birthday sleepover we'd been warned – on pain of death – not to wake her mum and dad up. With the baby they don't get much sleep. So even when we started to get really scared, we didn't dare go and get them. We just hid at the bottom of our sleeping bags. Well, so would you have done. Believe me, it was seriously scary.

Hang on. Before I tell you any more we'd better check no one's listening. My house isn't like Lyndz's. You can't be too careful round here. Walls have ears and so does my mum! Let's go down into the garden. If we see her, act natural. Be cool. My mum's a real Inspector Clouseau.

OK, you sit on the swing and I'll tell you the rest.

By the time her birthday came, Lyndz had managed to get round her mum and dad. They said yes, we could watch

Gremlins as long as...

1. It wasn't too scary. (Tom promised them it wasn't.)
2. It wasn't sexy. (P-lease!) (Tom told them it definitely wasn't.)
3. We all had our parents' permission. (Fliss wasn't going to be watching it, but she still needed permission, anyway.)
4. Lyndz paid for it out of her birthday money. (She said OK.)

And, most important of all:

5. If we scared ourselves out of our brains watching it, we'd better not keep them awake all night, or we wouldn't be worth a prayer!

"It's a deal," said Lyndz.

Then the rest of us had to persuade our parents. I thought it would be a piece of cake persuading mine. How wrong can you be?

"*Gremlins*?" said my mum. "I'm not sure about that. It's a 15, isn't it?"

"Fifteen! She'll be wanting to go to

raves next," said my dad.

"... and drinking..." said Mum.

"... and smoking."

My mum and dad think they're funny, but they're not. And they go on... and on...

"She'll be sniffing Pritt sticks..."

"... staying out all night..."

Honestly, what are they like? "It's only a video," I said. "Please!" I put on my most adorable Andrex-puppy face. I begged and pleaded and whined...

"All right! All right!" said Mum in the end. "Just this once."

Yeah! Four-one! I jumped up and smothered her with kisses.

"But I don't want you coming home feeling ill because you were too scared to sleep."

"Don't worry," I said. "You know me."

"Exactly," said Dad, "that's the trouble."

"Remember, you've been warned," said Mum.

I said, "Yeah, yeah. Hang loose,

Mother Goose," which always winds her up.

So I left, sharpish. 5-4-3-2-1 and I was gone, before they changed their minds.

Lyndz's birthday was on a Friday, so that day at school we were all OTT. Mrs Weaver threatened to split us up a couple of times if we couldn't settle down and get on with some work.

Kenny had got the OK from her parents. Fliss's mum had made her promise *on her life* that she wouldn't so much as peep at the screen, which is stupid because you couldn't have persuaded Fliss to watch it if you'd promised her a year's supply of Mint Magnums. Rosie's mum's pretty laid back so she hadn't taken too much persuading. We were so excited we were jumping up and down.

"I can't wait for tonight," I said.

"It's gonna be so cool," said Rosie.

"It's gonna be so scary," said Lyndz, grinning.

35

"I hope there's plenty of blood," said Kenny. "I do lurv a bit of blood!"

"I just hope," said Fliss, "that when you all scare yourselves out of your pants you'll remember that I was against this from the start."

Yawn, yawn. She can be so bor-ing.

"Don't worry, I don't scare easy," said Kenny.

"Oh, don't you *now*!" I shouted, suddenly frightening them all out of their wits. They just about jumped out of their seats. Mrs Weaver gave us a warning look.

"Don't do that," said Rosie. "I nearly wet myself."

"It isn't funny," said Fliss, white in the face.

"No, Francesca, it's very infantile," said Kenny, putting on Mrs Weaver's voice. "You wouldn't like it if someone scared you half to death, now would you?"

Well, no, I s'pose I wouldn't. Actually,

that night something did scare me half
to death and I didn't like it one little bit.

CHAPTER FIVE

Lyndz told us to come for six o'clock and when we got there her mum had made a brilliant spread: hot dogs (vegetarian for me and Lyndz), jacket potatoes, crisps, curry salad (not so good), egg and banana sandwiches (no, not together), milkshakes, toasted marshmallows, fairy cakes, oh and lots of cucumber.

Cucumber is one of our fave foods:

cucumber sandwiches, cubes of cucumber and cheese on sticks, cucumber salad and grated cucumber with yoghurt, with lots of salt on it. We don't mind how we eat it, as long as there's lots of cucumber.

After we'd eaten we got dressed up. I bagged a long silky dress with big sleeves like a pair of wings and silver shoes with heels. I would die for those shoes. Lyndz won't give them to me; I already asked her. So I always grab them first.

Kenny's in love with this purple velvet jacket and flared pants. She looked pretty weird because she was wearing them over her Leicester City Football Club T-shirt, which she just about lives in.

Rosie dressed up as a Strawberry Flower Fairy, Fliss was a mermaid and Lyndz wore her grandma's wedding dress, which Fliss wanted, but then she remembered that it *was* Lyndz's birthday.

Then we went to watch the film.

As a special treat, Lyndz had persuaded Stuart to let us use his room. He's got his own TV and video, so we could watch the film in there, rather than in the living room, which is packed out with things like new floorboards and radiators for Lyndz's bedroom. And, even better, he said we could *sleep* in his room.

Stuart has this humungous bed. Well, it isn't a proper bed with legs or anything, just this huge mattress on the floor. I wish my mum and dad would let me sleep on the floor. It's really cool. All of us fitted on it, and it was bouncy like a trampoline.

Stuart had gone to a rave at the Rugby Club and wouldn't be in till really late, so he said he'd sleep in Lyndz's bed, unless he stayed with one of his friends.

When Tom came in to set the video up for us, we were having a bouncing competition. I was winning, of course, because I'm so much bigger to start with. Once or twice I bounced into the lampshade.

"Right, are you lot ready?" said Tom.

We all did a few more bounces and then landed, sitting down in a row, facing the TV.

"Yeah! Good one!" shouted Kenny.

"Great timing," said Fliss.

"Synchronised bouncing!" I said. "That would make a brilliant new round for our International Gladiators contest."

"Stu must be mad," said Tom, shaking his head. "There's no way I'd let five weird women in my room. No way!"

"We're not women," Fliss giggled. "We're girls."

"And we're not weird," said Lyndz.

"That, little sister, is a matter of opinion. Are you sure you ought to watch this video? Isn't it a bit frightening for *little girls*?"

He grinned at us, but we all gave him

the evil eye and the cross of the vampire.

"Go away," said Lyndz.

"OK, OK, I'm going," he said, grinning. "But I may be back."

"Sssss," we hissed.

We all got comfy on Stuart's bed with our pillows behind us and a huge packet of popcorn between us. Fliss sat on her own, on a beanbag in the corner, with her back to the TV.

"Shall I turn it on?" said Lyndsey, with the remote ready in her hand.

"Not yet," said Fliss, taking out a green knitted hat and pulling it down over her face.

"You won't be able to breathe if you do that," said Lyndz.

"At least leave your mouth clear," said Rosie. "Then you can fit the popcorn in."

"She looks like a mugger," I whispered to Kenny.

"I heard that," said Fliss.

"Now are we ready?" said Lyndz.

"I'm not," said Rosie. "I need the loo."

I was glad Rosie had thought of it, because I knew I wouldn't dare go once the film had started. All the others must have thought the same, because then they all decided to go. But, at last, we really were ready.

We sat down on the bed close together, clutching hold of each other, grinning and squealing our heads off. And that was before Lyndz even switched it on!

Her dad put his head round the door, looking dead worried. "Are you lot all right?"

"It's OK, it hasn't started yet," said Lyndz.

"Well, just remember, we don't want you so overexcited you can't sleep. Is that understood?"

Yes, yes, we all nodded. We grinned at him. Lyndz said she'd had the same warning five times already that day.

Suddenly he spotted Fliss, sitting in the corner with a hood over her face.

"Felicity, are you sure you want to sit there like that all night? Why don't you come downstairs and watch something on TV?"

"No, it's all right, Dad," said Lyndz. "Fliss wants to stay with us."

"We're going to tell her what's happening," said Kenny.

"She just doesn't want to see it, that's all," I said.

Lyndz's dad shook his head. "And I thought boys were strange."

It was already quite dark. We couldn't decide whether to put the lights on or leave them off. It would be more spooky with them off, but we didn't want it *too spooky*. So we decided to keep Stuart's bedside light on, just in case.

You know! In case *anything* happened.

To tell you the truth, I was starting to feel a bit jumpy by now. Usually I don't mind the dark. I don't sleep with a light

on, like some people. But it's more scary
when you're in someone else's house. It
wouldn't have felt quite so scary in
Lyndz's room with all her horse pictures
around us. But we'd never been in
Stuart's room before.

I didn't say anything, though. I just
tried to be Ms Cool. Dead laid back.
Nothing worried me. Until the face at the
window!

CHAPTER SIX

I'm telling you, we nearly jumped out of our skin. It was seriously scary. We just looked over and there was this face pressed up against the glass. It looked gruesome.

"Oh, my God!" said Rosie. "What's that?"

Fliss whipped off her hood and started to scream. "Help! Help! Mummy! Mummy!"

"Shhh," said Lyndsey. "It's only my stupid brother. You're going to get it when Dad finds out you've been messing about with his ladders," she shouted at him through the glass. That's what Lyndz's brothers are like: always playing tricks on her.

"He nearly frit me to death," said Fliss.

Lyndsey pulled the curtains closed. Tom started tapping and making stupid howling noises. "Just ignore him," she said.

"I think we should open the window and push him off," said Kenny.

"I think we should empty a bucket of water over his head," I said.

"I think you should go and tell your dad," said Fliss.

"You know I can't do that," Lyndz reminded her. "I promised them: no trouble, or else."

So we did ignore him and finally he went away.

"Come on," said Kenny. "Are we ever

going to watch this film?"

We were all a bit shivery and we hadn't even seen a gremlin yet. At first, Rosie was right, they just seemed cute. It's going to be really tame, I thought. But was I wrong!

Some films are like that. They sort of trick you into thinking, This is OK, I can handle this. But then it changes and you feel as if you're on a roller coaster that's going too fast and you wish you could get off. One minute the gremlins were all cuddly and sweet, sort of burbling and singing, the next they were hissing and spitting and talking like Daleks and bursting out of wardrobes with lasers, attacking people.

A couple of times I almost jumped out of my skin. I tried to tell myself, This is only a film, it isn't really happening. Somebody made them up. They don't exist. There's no such thing as a gremlin. But then I began to think, What if there is? Right here, in this town, in Lyndz's street, in Stuart's bedroom? Ahhh! I buried my head in my knees.

I was glad Rosie had warned us about the bit with the microwave. When it came on, I didn't watch it. Kenny did, of course. She kept up a running commentary for Fliss.

"Now she's turned it on and it's going round and round in it. Now it's exploded. It's gone splat! all over the door. There's blood everywhere."

"Don't tell me that!" squealed Fliss. "It's gross! I don't want to hear any more."

So Kenny stopped telling her, but then, when she could still hear the rest of us groaning, she said, "What's happening now? What's going on? Somebody tell me what's happening." You can't win with Fliss.

There were lots of bits I had to watch with my hands in front of my face. Rosie kept burrowing into me and trying to hide between me and the wall. Lyndz hid her face in Stuart's pillow. Only Kenny watched all of it, but then you know what she's like.

When it got really hairy we had to turn the big light back on. We all kept our feet tucked right under us, even though there was no room for anything to be hiding under Stuart's bed, unless it was dead thin, like the Flat Man.

Some bits were pretty funny, actually, in a stupid way. But other bits were terrifying.

Every time we thought they'd killed the last one off, more of them would leap out of the dark. And that started us off screaming and grabbing hold of each other again.

The screaming was the best bit. I loved it. But I didn't like the gruesome bits. The people who think up horror films must have really weird minds. They were probably like Kenny when they were kids. Seriously weird.

CHAPTER SEVEN

Uh-oh, look out! There's Nathan from next door, looking over the fence. He seems to think just because I go there after school to be *minded* by his mum, he can barge in even when I've got friends round. Ignore him. He's stupid.

"Get a life, Nathan. Go away! This is girls' talk."

Come on, we'll go over the other side of the garden. This bit's not for *his* ears.

After the film had finished, we were really hot and sweating with all that squealing.

Lyndz's mum looked in to check on us. "Well, did you enjoy that?"

"It was wicked," said Kenny.

"Coo-el," I said.

"I just hope it's not going to give you nightmares."

"No, we're fine, Mum," said Lyndsey. "I promise."

"Well, I hope so. Now, can you hurry up in the bathroom? Because I'd like a bath before I go to bed and I'd like it before midnight."

But when she'd gone, still nobody moved. I guess no one wanted to go down that long corridor from Stuart's room and right round the corner to the bathroom on their own. What if there were gremlins hiding behind the curtains, waiting at the top of the stairs, lurking in the bathroom? So we all started to get ready for bed instead.

The most important part of your sleepover kit is your sleeping bag and your pillow. Mine's a special one with Winnie-the-Pooh and Piglet walking in the snow on the pillowcase. It's not my regular pillow, it's an old one, so I'm allowed to use it for pillow fights. Kenny used to have an inflatable one. We used to blow it up really hard and sit on it, so the air rushed out and made rude noises, like a whoopee cushion. But once she blew it up so hard it burst. Now she has an ordinary one like the rest of us.

Stuart's bed was so big we could all fit on it but there was only room for four of us in a row, so someone had to sleep across the bottom with everyone's feet resting on them. We had a pillow fight to see who.

We swung them round and whacked each other with them and tried to knock each other off the bed. The last person left on the bed was the winner. We were right in the middle of it – Fliss and Rosie had been knocked out – when Lyndz's mum popped her head in and out.

"This is absolutely your *last* call for the bathroom," she said.

"OK, Mum," said Lyndsey.

We all flopped down on the mattress, exhausted.

"I'm too tired to move," said Kenny. "I think I'll stay mucky."

None of us likes washing much. It seems a waste of time being in the bathroom when you could be having a laugh with your friends.

"Oh, dear," I said, sniffing the air. "What is that odour?" I sniffed a path all the way to Kenny, like a bloodhound. "Ugh. Disgusting!"

"*You're* disgusting," said Fliss. She thinks it's so rude, talking about people smelling; the rest of us think it's a real laugh.

I pretended the smell had made me

faint and I rolled over on top of Kenny.

"Watch my bladder," she squealed. "I really need to go."

"Bladder!" said Lyndsey and started to shriek. "Bladder!"

Kenny just rolled her eyes and gave us a look. She's going to be a doctor, like her dad, when she grows up. She's always using words like "bladder".

"Well, go, if you want to go," said Fliss. But Kenny still didn't move.

None of us really wanted to go to bed. We wanted to keep the lights on and play all night. But it was late, nearly eleven o'clock. We started to get undressed.

When we get undressed at a sleepover, we always do it inside our sleeping bags. We wriggle down inside with our jimjams, then throw out our clothes, like we're doing the fastest striptease in the world, only no one can see us because we're inside our sleeping bags. Kenny's usually the fastest; I'm usually the last because I'm so big and, like my grandma says, all arms and legs and feet.

But the moment Lyndz crawled down into hers, she started screaming and scrambled out as if there was an alligator at the bottom. "Ugh, ugh! What's that?" she squealed.

Out came Buster, their little Jack Russell terrier. He's always curling up in funny places and going to sleep. He looked pretty annoyed to be woken up.

The poor dog ran to the door and whined to be let out.

"It was horrible!" said Lyndz. "I could feel something soft and warm and then he started licking my feet and it felt wet and yukky."

"It must have been far worse for him," I said, "having your big smelly feet land on his head."

Kenny found something at the bottom of hers too, but it was only her torch.

"Brillo! I thought I'd lost that. I've

been looking for it all week," she said.

She turned it on and held it under her chin. She pulled a terrible face and then said, in a creepy voice, "I know, let's read a scary story."

We always bring a scary book with us to sleepovers, but we'd read most of them before, and after that film they seemed pretty tame. So we decided to tell our own stories. Looking back on it now, we should have listened to Fliss.

"I don't want to do this," she said. "I might be sick."

"You won't be sick," said Rosie.

"Well, I'll have nightmares," she said. But Kenny said she couldn't have nightmares if she didn't go to sleep, and if she wanted we'd all stay awake with her.

After all, the whole point of sleepovers is *not* to go to sleep, isn't it?

"I still don't want to," said Fliss.

"Oh come on," said Kenny.

"Don't worry, we'll all be together,"

said Lyndz. "It'll be a laugh."

"You'll be all right," I said. "You can come in the middle, if you like."

So she dragged her sleeping bag between us and we got in really close around her.

"Someone put the light out," said Kenny.

"Do we have to have the light out?" Fliss started to whinge.

"Yes," said Kenny. "It won't be as good if we don't. We've got our torches."

So we all turned on our torches. I put out the light and then dived back into my place.

Lyndz said, "Frankie, you start."

"OK," I said. "Snuggle up close."

I could feel the others round me, shivering with excitement. It was wonderful. It felt scary, but in a good way – to begin with. But somehow things got a bit out of hand – well, more than a bit, actually.

CHAPTER EIGHT

Even if I say so myself, I tell the best stories. My gran says it's because I'm a bit of an actress. And I suppose I am. I'd love to be in films or on TV. I try to do it like our teacher, Mrs Weaver. She tells us brill stories, with all the voices and lots of expression. Not like Mr Short, our last teacher. He used to talk down his nose. He was bor-ing. We used to fall asleep when he read us anything.

But I do all the voices. I'm especially good at creepy voices. I know when to whisper and then, when everyone's leaning forward so they can hear, I suddenly shout and make them jump out of their skins, just when they're not expecting it.

I looked over my shoulder, as if *something* was already in the room with us, lurking in the shadows. I lowered my voice and whispered, "Prepare to meet ... the Blur!"

"Uh-oh," said Lyndsey, grinning. "Not the Blur!"

"Oh, no," said Fliss. "I don't like this."

"Shhhh," said the others.

The Blur is this character I invented. "It doesn't have a face," I told them, "it's just this shape that can pass through walls. It can slide through anything, even bullet-proof glass.

"Sometimes, when you think you've seen something out of the corner of your eye and then you look again real

60

quick, and it's gone, that was the Blur."

"That's how fast it moves, like a flash. It just glides through anything and then hides, like a shape-shifter, pretending to be something ordinary and harmless. It might be hiding behind the curtains, or in the corner of the stairs, or behind the toilet door, or under your bed, or even in the bottom of your sleeping bag. It might be waiting for you right now," I said, dropping my voice even lower. "So be careful, or it might jump out and *get you*!"

"Don't *do* that!" said Fliss. "You'll make me sick."

"Yeah," said Lyndz. "You nearly scared me to death."

Rosie was clutching her throat. "Honestly, Frankie, you could have warned us."

"That was wicked," said Kenny. "My turn next. Erm, let me think…"

She shone her torch under her chin so that her whole face glowed, and when she grinned her eyes disappeared into two little slits. You could still tell it was Kenny, but she looked too ugly to live. It was gruesome. I could hardly bear to look at her.

"I know," she said. "I'll tell you about the Ghost Train."

I've heard this story before. Kenny's sister told it to her. She'd heard it at school. There's a little low bridge that goes over the railway line on Arthur Street. Well, years and years ago there was a big crash there and a train ploughed into the side of the bridge and every single person on the train was killed. Sometimes you're supposed to be able to hear the train whistle in the distance. And some people say that if you stay there until it comes under the bridge, you'll see it go by, full of ghosts.

Then you have to look away, really quickly because if they look you in the eye they'll pull you on board and then you'll turn into a ghost and be stuck on the train for ever.

Kenny started making ghost noises, but it sounded more like a steam train. We all started to giggle, but we soon stopped, because there was a knock on the wall.

"What was that?" said Fliss. "Oooh! I don't like it."

"It's OK," said Lyndz, putting her arm round Fliss's shoulders.

I said, "It's probably the Blur, knocking to come in." I grinned at Kenny. I guessed it was her knocking. We often play that game. But this time she looked back and shook her head as if it wasn't. Then there was another knock.

Rosie said, "Perhaps it's the Grey Lady, trying to make contact with us."

Do you ever play that game: White Lady, Grey Lady? Sometimes we throw a stone in the air and ask her questions. Or sometimes we knock on the floor and talk to her.

"Ask her something," said Lyndz.

I looked at Kenny. She still wasn't grinning, but she nodded.

"Is there anybody there?" I said in my spooky talking-to-ghosts voice. "Knock once for yes, twice for no."

"That's stupid," said Fliss. "How can she knock twice if she isn't there?"

"Shhh," said the others.

There was one knock.

"Ask her something else," said Rosie. "Ask if she's a friend."

"If you're a friend, knock once," I said. "If you're an enemy, knock twice."

There was one loud knock. We were all glad about that.

"Have you got a message for us?" I asked. "Knock once for yes."

There was another knock.

"Who's it for?" said Rosie.

I said, "If it's for me, Francesca Theresa Thomas, knock once. If it's for Rosie Cartwright, knock twice. If it's for Lyndsey Collins, knock three times. If it's for Kenny, I mean Laura McKenzie, knock four times. And if it's for Felicity Sidebotham, knock five times."

There was a long row of knocks.

"Five," gasped Lyndz. "It's for Fliss."

"I don't want it," said Fliss, wriggling down into her sleeping bag. "Tell her to go away. I don't want any messages." She was getting really worked up.

"Ask if she's got a message for someone else," said Rosie.

But I felt a bit like Fliss. I didn't really want to know. It's OK when you play games like this at school, in the daytime, but not in the dark. And I still couldn't work out who was doing the knocking, so I was starting to get a bit nervous. Rosie nudged me.

"Is there a message for anyone else?" I said.

There was no knock this time. We sat waiting in the torchlight for what seemed like ages. I could feel Lyndz holding on to me on one side and I could feel Fliss's nails digging into my other arm. We were all holding our breath, wondering what was going to happen. Kenny was grinning, but then she often does that when she's really nervous. It gets her into loads of bother at school. I started to shiver.

Suddenly the bedroom door flew open and in walked this tall lady.

CHAPTER NINE

She wasn't in grey, she was all in white, from the top of her head to her feet. Thank goodness, it was Lyndsey's mum in a long, white dressing gown with a towel round her hair. We nearly died of fright.

"Whatever's going on?" she said. "Who keeps knocking? You'll wake the baby up."

"It wasn't me, honest, Mum," said

Lyndsey. She looked at the rest of us, but no one spoke. We just shrugged and looked at each other.

I knew it wasn't me; I knew it wasn't Fliss. It had to be one of the other three leaning against the wall. But none of them owned up.

Lyndz's mum looked really fed up with us. "Fancy sitting here in the dark, after a film like that. I knew this would happen. You'll never get to sleep tonight, I can tell."

"We will, honest," said Lyndsey. "We're going to sleep now, Mum."

"I want no more knocking. Now, put those torches away and settle down, do you hear?"

"Yes, Mum."

"Good night."

We all muttered, "Good night."

She closed the door and we heard her go back to bed. We snuggled down into our sleeping bags and lay in the dark without a sound.

"I think we'd better go to sleep," Lyndz whispered.

"OK," Kenny whispered back.

"Good night," whispered Fliss.

We heard the church clock strike midnight. There wasn't a sound from the others. I really tried to go to sleep, but I just couldn't settle. *We still hadn't been to the bathroom.*

I couldn't wait any longer and I was about to say so when Fliss's voice came through the dark. "I'm dying for a wee and I'm too scared to go on my own."

"So am I."

"And me."

"I'm bursting," said Kenny. "It's giving me a pain."

"Let's all go together," I said.

We started to get out of our sleeping bags.

"What if there's anything out there?" said Fliss.

"What, like the Blur, you mean?" said Lyndz.

"Or gremlins," whispered Fliss.

"Gremlins aren't real," I said.

"But what if they are?"

"*They aren't!*" I insisted. "Now come on, let's stick together. Let's hold hands."

As we crept out of the bedroom, I was last and I grabbed hold of Stuart's tennis racquet, propped against the wall, just in case.

Yes, I know I told Fliss gremlins aren't real, but you can't be too careful.

We made our way along the landing to the bathroom in the little bit of light that shone through the landing window. We couldn't risk waking anyone by putting a light on. We'd have been in doom for ever.

Of course when we got there we had this big argument, in whispers, about who was going in first. Lyndz told us to be quiet or her mum would hear us, and anyway she was going in first, because *it was her birthday!*

I said, "It isn't, *actually*, it's gone midnight." But she'd already slipped in and closed the door.

By the time we'd hung around on the landing until *everyone* had been, we'd all got really cold in our jimjams and bare feet. So when we got back to the bedroom, we couldn't stop shaking. Fliss said she was feeling a bit sick and by now so was I.

It could have been all the popcorn we'd eaten. It could have been watching *Gremlins*. It could have been nearly jumping out of our skins when Lyndz's mum came in. Whatever it was, we were all starting to feel funny.

"Perhaps we'd better go to sleep," said Lyndz. "Fliss looks terrible."

She did. She was a funny green colour and her eyes had sunk into her head.

"OK," I said.

"I'm dead beat anyway," said Kenny.

"Yes, let's all go to sleep," said Rosie. But it wasn't that easy.

When it's a sleepover, we all have different ways of getting to sleep and we never agree on it. But the one thing we *always* do before we settle down is to sing our song. We have this sort of club song and we sit up in our sleeping bags and do it with the hand movements. I bet you know it.

"Down by the river there's a hanky-pankyyy,
With a bull-frog sitting near the hanky-pankyyy.
With an ooh-ah, ooh-ah, hey, Mrs Zippy, with a 1-2-3 OUT!"

And the first one to lie down flat on the word OUT! turns off her torch. Then we keep on going round until everyone's out. No one likes being last because then you're left sitting there almost in the dark and it's a bit creepy. That night it felt mega-creepy.

Fliss was the last one and then she

wouldn't turn her torch off because she said she was too scared to go to sleep unless the light was on. The trouble is, I can't get to sleep unless the light's out. So I made Fliss turn it off.

Kenny likes to hum to herself and make sort of snuffling noises. It drives her sister, Molly the Monster, mad. *And* she talks in her sleep. She says some potty things.

Rosie's just like our dog. When Pepsi wants to lie down, she has this funny routine where she goes round and round in circles scruffing up her bed until it's just how she likes it and then she flops down, curled up in a ball. Rosie does that. She tries out every position she can think of before she settles. She starts off on her back, then she turns on one side, then the other, then she rolls over on her stomach. We thought she was never going to settle down. We all yelled, "Rosie! Cut it out."

It was like trying to sleep on a bouncy castle.

The next thing, Fliss started to sniff. Then Kenny started up and then they all seemed to be playing pass the sniff.

"Pack it in," I said.

There was another sniff.

"Fliss!"

"It wasn't me," she said. "It must have been Kenny."

"It was not. It was Rosie."

There was one humongus sniff. "Sorry, sorry," said Fliss. "That *was* me. But I won't do it again. I've finished, honest."

Finally everyone was quiet. I was just dropping off when I heard Kenny say, "By the way, who was it, knocking on the wall?"

Suddenly I was wide awake. "I thought it was you," I said.

"It must have been Rosie."

Rosie said, "I thought it was Frankie."

"I'll bet it was Lyndz," said Kenny.

"Not guilty. Must have been Fliss."

"*It wasn't me!*" Fliss almost shrieked.

We all sat up in bed and turned our torches back on.

"So who was it? Come on, own up."

"*You* own up," said Fliss. "You're the one who does that kind of thing."

"Look, I'm telling the truth." And I licked my finger and made a cross on my chest. "Cross my heart and hope to die," I said.

So then everyone else licked their fingers, crossed their hearts and made the Brownie sign as well. Well, someone must be telling porky pies and I was going to find out who. I stared them in the eye, one by one. But this time no one blinked.

CHAPTER
TEN

I don't know about you, but I hate mysteries. At least, I hate ones I can't solve. And then what I hate is that I can't stop thinking about them. You know what it's like when someone asks you if you can remember the words to a song or the name of a book or a character in it, and you can't. After a while they say, oh, never mind, and they just forget about it, but then *you* can't. And it drives you mad until you can remember. That happens to me all the time. My dad says it's because I'm stubborn and I won't let go of things.

Well, now I couldn't let go of this. I went through the possibilities. I *knew* it wasn't me knocking. I was *sure* it wasn't Fliss. It *wasn't* Lyndz, she would have owned up. So that left Rosie and Kenny. It could have been Kenny. I know she sometimes tells porkies, for a laugh, but she *usually* owns up in the end. So it must have been Rosie. I looked straight into her eyes, as if I could see inside her head and read her mind like a book. I was staring so hard my eyes began to water.

"Stop it," said Fliss. "You're frightening me."

"Yeah, pack it in," said Lyndz.

"I'm going to get to the bottom of this," I said, "because if it wasn't any of us knocking, you know what that means. It means that this house... is *haunted*."

But before any of them could speak, we heard noises: stairs creaking, footsteps coming along the landing, then stopping outside the bedroom door...

"Quick," whispered Lyndz. "It might be my mum."

We all put out our torches and lay down and pulled our sleeping bags over our heads and pretended to be fast asleep.

By now we were covered in goose bumps. We lay there waiting for the footsteps to go away, waiting for Lyndz's mum or dad to go back to bed, but they didn't. They just stood there for a moment.

Then, slowly, the door handle started to turn and the door started to open.

"Oh, help!" whispered Fliss. "I want my mum."

I wanted mine too. I slid down inside my sleeping bag and tried to block up my ears so I couldn't hear the next thing, but the room was so quiet you could have heard a feather drop.

Then there was the loudest hiccup I'd ever heard, or it could have been a burp. Something or somebody tripped over and fell headlong into the room and sprawled across the carpet. A funny deep voice said, "Who's that sleeping in my bed?"

It sounded just like one of the three bears. I thought, I've heard that voice before. I dared myself to look just as everyone else sat up and started squealing.

"Shhh, shhh!" hissed Lyndsey, turning on the light.

Lying there on the floor was her stupid brother. Not her stupid brother Tom, who'd already nearly given us forty fits with his face at the window. No, this was her other stupid brother, Stuart. He was lying on his back, grinning. His face was red and he looked sort of…

"Drunk! You're drunk," said Lyndz. "Stuart, get up this minute or I'll go and tell Dad. You're supposed to be sleeping in *my* bed."

"Oh, yes," he said, looking as if he could vaguely remember that arrangement. "Sorry," he mumbled. But he made no move. He just lay there on his back, like a whale. Then he closed his eyes and started snoring.

"Get up!" said Lyndsey. She crawled behind him and propped him up. He blinked, looked around and saw us all watching him, our eyes nearly out on stalks.

"Don't worry," he mumbled. "You all go back to sleep. I'll just go along to Lyndz's room." He rolled over onto all fours and sort of dragged himself up to a standing position. "Didn't mean to scare you." He swayed a bit and then, when he was steady enough, he backed out of the door and tiptoed along the landing. "Good night."

After he'd gone, we sat there for a minute staring at each other before anyone spoke. None of us had ever really seen anyone drunk before.

"I can't believe your brothers," I said.

"They're maniacs," said Kenny.

"They're idiots," said Rosie.

"Don't worry," said Lyndz. "They'll pay for it. Both of them." She started to think of all the things she could make them do for her: clean her riding boots, give her extra pocket money, take her turn at emptying the compost bucket. "If Dad finds out about this, he'll have fifty thousand fits. They'll be my slaves for weeks after this."

Now the excitement was over, Fliss said, "I think I'm going to be sick."

Fliss is always saying she's going to be sick. The trouble is, sometimes she is. We didn't know if this was one of those times. She certainly looked strange, but then we were all looking pretty strange by now.

"You'll be OK," said Lyndz. "If you just get to sleep, you'll be fine."

"I don't think I can get to sleep," she wailed.

"We'll help you," said Rosie. "We'll tell you a story."

"No more stories!" said Fliss. "It was probably those that made me feel sick in the first place."

"You need to take your mind off it. Think about something else."

"Like what?" said Fliss.

"Pistachio ice cream," said Lyndz.

Fliss sort of gulped and turned green. "P-lease."

Then I started to giggle, because I couldn't think of many things that looked more like a bowl of sick than pistachio ice cream. Kenny must have had the same idea because she started pretending to throw up. Then we all joined in. It was so stupid even Fliss burst out laughing.

"You're disgusting," she said. But she was starting to look better already.

"I'm hungry," said Lyndz. "We haven't had our midnight feast yet."

That was true, we hadn't. We'd all been so busy scaring ourselves silly, we'd forgotten about eating.

We heard the church clock down the road strike two o'clock as we sat there eating Black Jacks, Opal Fruits and Monster Munches. It was magic.

Then we snuggled down and turned out the lights and took it in turns to tell Fliss jokes, to keep her mind off feeling sick.

The last thing I remember was Kenny saying, "What do you give an elephant with big feet?"

And Rosie yawning and saying, "Lots of room."

Super stars!

GOODBYE

The next morning none of us could wake up. Even Lyndz slept in.

"Whatever time did you girls get to sleep?" Lyndz's mum asked us.

"Don't know," said Lyndz. "Didn't see the clock." Which was sort of true.

We were all feeling sick. No one could eat any breakfast. Lyndz's mum was really worried about Fliss. She still looked a funny colour. I felt *terrible*. But when my mum and dad came to collect me, I tried to pretend I was OK.

I gave them a big smile, but it felt as if my face was going to crack.

"Are you all right?" they asked, dead suspicious.

"Yeah," I said, lying through my teeth.

"Did you have a good time?"

"Yeah." But I couldn't keep it up. In fact, as soon as the car started, I was sick all over the back seat. So that was that. Mega trouble.

I told them it was probably the curry salad but they didn't believe me.

In fact, I haven't had a very nice week at all. I missed school on Monday and every day I keep on thinking about gremlins jumping out of cupboards and swinging from the lights and hiding under my bed. Scar-y.

But the good thing is, I suddenly remembered Winnie the Pooh. I was looking for something really cosy and safe to read in bed and I suddenly thought of Pooh and Piglet. I've reread all the stories and all the poems this week. It's nice, isn't it, finding old friends you'd forgotten? It's a good job I did, because I'm not allowed out.

Yep, grounded again. Just my luck. But so are all the others. Anyway, in the end, Lyndz let it out at home about Stuart coming home drunk, so he got in trouble with their dad, then she got in trouble with Stuart for telling on him.

But at least Lyndz found out it was Tom who'd been knocking on the wall, so that cleared up that mystery. Aren't brothers gruesome? We won't forget Lyndz's birthday sleepover in a hurry.

So, listen, take my advice, if you're going to watch a scary video, don't sit up telling horror stories *and* talking to ghosts *and* eating midnight feasts until two in the morning. Not if you want to keep in your parents' good books.

Uh-oh. There's my mum, looking for me now. I'd better go in before I get into any more trouble.

Remember: don't tell anyone what I've told you.

Now you've finished the book... eat it. See ya.

theres alot of things
a super stars

can do!!!

Theres a lot of Things super
Stars canaol!,!

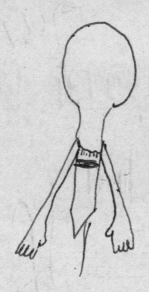

The Sleepover Club
at Felicity's

QUICK,
THE TOASTER'S ON FIRE!

CHAPTER ONE

Come on, let's go up to my bedroom. My mum's got visitors coming round and she's having a bit of a spring clean. She only gets the Hoover out once in a blue moon, but when she does – look out! She's dangerous.

Dad's in the kitchen making pizza. Do you like pizza? I adore it. I could eat it every day. Come to think of it, I do eat it *almost* every day. That's because it's my dad's speciality. Mum says she married him for his pizza. I wouldn't marry any of the boys I know, even if they made the

9

best pizza in the entire universe. But then I'm not getting married. No way. Not ever.

None of us is interested in boys, except Fliss, of course, but that's only because she's so soppy about weddings. And Ryan Scott. Yuk!

Uh-oh. The Hoover's stopped and I can hear my mum shouting.

"Francesca! I hope you're getting on with your homework."

"Nearly finished, Mum."

"Well, you're not going out until it's done."

"I know."

Better keep our voices down. Mum's on the warpath. She's still in a razz over the *Cooking Incident*. That was so cool. Killing, in fact. Well, it wasn't so funny for Kenny; she broke her arm in two places. But even she says it was worth it. Fliss's nosy neighbours weren't very happy, but then we don't really care what *they* think.

Fliss did care at first. She nearly went haywire. She thought she'd be in doom for ever with her mum and Andy. But in the end even they saw the funny side of it.

The bad news is, we all got banned from cooking, ever again! And you know what that means: none of us can win the Brownie Cook's Challenge. Now one of the crummy M&Ms will win it. They're our biggest enemies: Emma Hughes and Emily Berryman. They're in our class at school and they are seriously gruesome, but there you go. As my grandma says, life's very unfair, especially for children.

I wasn't telling porkies, you know: I have *nearly* done my homework, 'A Day in the Life of a Viking'. Bor-ing. Just sit and wait for me while I finish it and then we'll go round to Kenny's. On the way I'll tell you what happened at our last sleepover. All the juicy details.

Come on, we'll walk through the new estate; it's the quickest way to Kenny's.

Kenny's the crazy one. Her real name's Laura McKenzie.

I've told you about Fliss already, Felicity *Sidebotham*. She hates that name.

Lyndz and Rosie may be there as well, then you'll have met all of us: the whole Sleepover Club, the Fearless Five, as my dad calls us.

And I'm Frankie, the most fearless of all. Yeah! Well, sometimes.

OK, so where shall I start? I suppose it all started the day Fliss called Lyndz 'fat'. Oh boy, was she mad!

We were sitting in the dining hall at school eating lunch; at our school they separate the packed lunches from the school dinners in case the dinner people catch something nasty like mad-tuna disease or cheese-and-pickle poisoning. Anyway, it suits me because I'm vegetarian and I'd rather not sit and watch people eating dead animals, thank you very much. Kenny doesn't mind what she eats; she's a real carnivore. She likes minced mad-cow burgers. Ugh!

One day the dreaded M&Ms came and

sat by Kenny when she was eating roast pork. Emily Berryman said, "Ooh, you've got pig's bottom on your plate." Kenny just lifted her plate and put it under Berryman's nose and said, "You'd better smell it, then."

Well, that spelled t-r-o-u-b-l-e. The plate went flying across the room and both of them spent the dinner hour standing outside Mrs Poole's door.

The moral of that story is: don't tangle with Kenny. She can be pretty wild.

But back to the story.

Lyndz opened her lunchbox and inside she had one of those new desserts. You know those Choc-pots? I love that kind of thing but my mum never buys them. She says they're nothing but sugar and I'll thank her when I'm fifty and I've still got all my own teeth. P-lease!

But Fliss looked at it and said, "Do you know how many calories there are in those?"

Yawn, yawn. Fliss is always turning into

an expert on something. At the moment it's *diets*. She so *stoopid*. I talked to my mum about it; she nearly went ballistic.

"Dieting's very bad for children. You'd better not let me hear *you* talking about counting calories. Growing girls meed plenty of healthy food..."

"Yeah, yeah," I told her. "I know that. It's Fliss who needs the lecture not me."

I did try to tell Fliss but she wouldn't listen. Well, not at first, anyway. She just went on pinching titchy bits of skin between her fingers and saying, "Oh, I'm getting so fat." Which is ridiculous. She looks like one of those stick insects Mr Short keeps in a tank in his classroom. Her mum's dead slim as well, but it doesn't stop her doing all these potty diets where you only eat nuts and fruit for a week. We told Fliss she didn't need to do *that* diet, she's a fruit and nut case already.

Well, at first Lyndz just ignored her and scoffed into her yummy Choc–pot. But then Fliss said, "You'll get even fatter eating things like that, you know."

Uh-oh. That put the king in the cake.

"What do you mean *even fatter*?" Lyndz nearly spat out the words. "I'm not fat."

Fliss just smiled and looked away as if something absolutely fascinating was going on at the next table.

"I'm *not* fat," Lyndz said again.

"Of course you're not fat," I said, and Rosie agreed with me. But Lyndz put down her spoon and stopped eating.

That was just the start of it. She spent the rest of the day asking everyone, over and over, "Do *you* think I'm fat? Honestly? Do you? Tell me the truth."

It didn't seem to make a scrap of difference that we all *were* telling the truth. Fliss had really got her worried. The M&Ms came round stirring things up, hanging round our table puffing out their cheeks and rolling their eyes, looking like a pair of bull-frogs. Lyndz was nearly in tears.

The point is, Lyndz *isn't* skinny like

Fliss and me. I'm a walking flagpole, all arms and legs and long fingers. By the way, do you like this nail varnish? It's called Silver Frost. Isn't it drastic? But I can't help being thin, it's just the way I am. Kenny's not that thin and Rosie's sort of in-between, just ordinary. Lyndz is just a bit rounder, that's all. She's got these cute little creases in her cheeks when she smiles. She's got them in her knees as well. I call them happy knees because they sort of smile at you.

But fat she is not. Absolutely, definitely, not on your life is she fat.

After that, though, she'd got it into her head that she was and there was nothing we could do to persuade her otherwise.

Every lunchtime for the rest of the week she and Fliss would sit there reading the back of a crisp packet or a pot of yoghurt to see how many calories were in it. I was getting seriously bored with it all. I mean, I'm interested in food but not in diets.

They're so stupid. It was bad enough at lunchtime, but when we were planning our next sleepover and they started talking about what we could and couldn't eat for our midnight feast, I thought, this has gone *too far*!

"No chocolate," said Fliss, "and none of those cheesy snacks, they're loaded. No popcorn…"

I couldn't believe my ears. "Oh, get a life," I said.

"You can't have a midnight feast without chocolate," said Rosie.

"Cucumber's OK," said Fliss. "There aren't any calories in cucumber."

"Oh, big fat hairy deal," said Kenny.

"No, *small thin* hairy deal, actually," I said.

We both cracked up. But by now it had gone past a joke. It was getting serious.

CHAPTER TWO

The thing is, we all love food. It's one of our fave things. Next to sleepovers, that is. We've all been practising for our Cook's badge at Brownies. And we were going to have this cooking contest. It was Brown Owl's idea. Now she's got back with her boyfriend, she's really cheered up again and we're doing some neat things. We've taken ages to do our Help at Home Challenge, so she suggested, to liven it up, we'd have this little competition.

There's eight of us doing it: the five of

us, the crummy M&Ms and Alana Banana Palmer. We know she won't win, for a start. She couldn't cook to save her life. Whenever she pours the squash out, only half of it goes in the cups.

Brown Owl said, "You can make one thing each – anything, you can choose. You can have a bit of help at home, but it has to be your own work."

I knew straight off what I was going to make, but I kept it quiet.

"I'm making butterfly cakes with buttercream filling," said Fliss. "They're my best."

"Oh, listen to Ready Steady Cook," said Kenny. "What are you making, Frankie?"

"I'm not telling," I said.

"Ooh-er! Get her!" said Kenny. "Classified information. You will not make me speak."

I reminded them it was supposed to be a competition.

"All right. If *you're* not telling, I'm not telling, either," said Fliss.

Rosie pointed out she already had.

"Well, I can change my mind."

So then everyone got dead secretive, which wasn't easy because we're all hopeless at keeping secrets from each other.

Anyway, after that, we were cooking mad. Every time I rang Kenny up, she was too busy to talk to me because she was in the kitchen making some *gruesome mess*, according to her sister Molly. And Fliss kept rabbiting on about these wonderful *novel cuisine* recipes she was making with her mum.

"I don't think that's right," I said. "I think it's *nouvelle cuisine*. It's French."

"Well, my mum calls it *novel cuisine*, so it must be."

This is something else you should know about Fliss: she and her mum are always right.

"My mum hardly lets me do any cooking," moaned Rosie. "She says she's got enough work to do without rescuing my disasters. I have to wait until she goes out, then Tiff lets me have a go." Tiff is Rosie's older sister. She's fifteen, almost a grown-up. "It's not fair. She makes me do all the boring bits like washing and drying the pots, looking after Adam, walking the dog, doing the errands –"

"Oh, poor little thing!" said Kenny, winding her up. "I should ring Childline."

But it's true, Rosie does have to do a lot at home, especially for Adam, her brother, who's in a wheelchair and needs a bit of looking after.

"Oh, my mum lets me do anything," said Fliss, bragging again. "I can make anything I want. But my best recipe is ..." And she smiled that *stoopid* smile she wears sometimes. "Oh, gosh, I nearly told you and spoiled the big secret."

She was just trying to get me going. I knew that, so I ignored her.

And I managed to keep my secret all week, which is some kind of record for me. I suppose I can tell you, though. Not that it's a secret any more. I was going to make pizza. The truth is, I couldn't think what else to make. My dad only cooks pizza and pancakes. My mum doesn't really cook much at all. She says she's a liability in the kitchen. And they both work such long hours that they don't have much time for cooking.

We don't eat only pizza and pancakes; we have lots of nice food from the supermarket. My mum says we should have shares in Marks & Spencer.

My dad says he's probably the world's best chef – at warming things up. "I might write a book on it," he says. "It's very skilled, you know."

He puts on mum's apron and gives us a cookery demonstration, from the best way to open the packaging right down to how to serve it on the plates. He's really silly. My mum says, "Cut out the clever stuff, just read the packet and follow the instructions. We're starving here."

That's one of the reasons I love going

to Kenny's house, because her mum does lots of home cooking. You can smell it the minute you go in the house. Ahhhh, Bisto! You know what I mean?

But once Fliss and Lyndz got started on calorie-counting, everyone seemed to lose interest in our cooking contest. It was the same boring conversation every time food was mentioned. Until I had a brainwave.

We were sitting round our table at school while Mrs Weaver was taking the register.

"I've got this great idea," I said.

"Oh, she's so modest," said Kenny.

"No, listen. We could all do some cooking for the sleepover on Friday. It would be a great chance to practise. We could all make something for our midnight feast."

"Good idea, Batman," said Kenny. The others all agreed too.

"Yeah, great," said Fliss. "We'll finally get to see what big secret Frankie's been

23

cooking up." And she gave me one of her sideways looks.

"I know what Frankie's cooking up," said Kenny. "Pizza."

I was fizzing mad. How did she know?

"Oh, yeah," said Fliss. "Of course, the famous Thomas pizza."

I didn't like the way Fliss said that. I knew she was just jealous. I was proud of my dad's pizza and I didn't want her making fun of it.

"I suppose you'll be making something without any *calories* in it," I snapped back.

"It won't be butterfly cakes with buttercream filling, then," said Kenny.

"Oh, no way," I said. "They're *loaded*."

Fliss went bright pink. She hadn't thought of that.

"Well, there's plenty of nice low-calorie things you can make, aren't there, Lyndsey?"

Lyndz's shoulders sagged. She didn't look as if she could think of any.

The others started talking about what they were going to make, but I kept quiet. I was annoyed because Kenny had blown my secret. But it was too late to change my mind. It would have to be pizza. I'd already asked my dad to teach me and we'd had a couple of lessons. In fact, we were having another one on Friday, just before the sleepover.

That was when I decided to talk to my mum about this stupid diet stuff.

CHAPTER THREE

Me and Dad were in the kitchen, cooking. Mum was washing up. We'd made the pizza dough and it was still rising. So we were slicing the cheeses to go on top. We were making four-cheese pizza, which is my fave topping, and I'd asked my dad if I could take some for our midnight feast.

"Pizza at midnight?" he said. "You'll all be sick!"

"They'd better not be," said Mum, "or Nikki'll have something to say about that."

Nikki is Fliss's mum and she is mega-

26

houseproud.

"We won't be sick," I told them.

"Well, OK," said Dad. "We'd better make an extra-big one if we're going to feed all those gannets. I've never known girls eat like you lot do."

"Mum," I said, "do you think Lyndz is fat?"

"Fat!" she said. "Oh, Francesca, don't be silly."

"Fliss told Lyndz she was getting fat and now she keeps going on about diets and calories and inch for pinch and things."

"I've told you before about that," said Mum. "Dieting's bad for you. Especially for growing children. I should think Lyndsey's mum would be very cross if she knew about it. I thought you girls had more sense."

"I *have*," I said.

"People are different," said Dad. "We're not all meant to be thin."

"I know that," I told them. "It was Fliss

who started it. It was nothing to do with me."

"Well, it is to do with you, Francesca, because they're your friends. So *you'd* better talk to them and sort it out."

Just like that, as if it was the easiest thing in the world. Sometimes my mum talks to me as if there's nothing I can't do. It's quite scary really.

"OK. Time to stretch the dough," said Dad.

That's the best bit, where you swing the dough round on your fists. It's ace. It's nearly as good as tossing pancakes. Dad's brilliant at it. I'm not, yet; I usually put my fingers through it.

"You just need plenty of practice," Dad said.

"Oh, joy," said Mum. She was up to her elbows in the washing-up at the time. Good job I knew she was joking. Well, I think she was.

Afterwards, when the pizza was in the oven, I thought about what Mum had said. I didn't know what to do. I needed a plan of action. So I rang Kenny. I always ring Kenny if I want to work something out. I always think better through my mouth, if you know what I mean.

"Hi, Kenny."

"Hiya."

"Hello. Who's that?"

"Molly, get off the extension. It's Frankie for me."

"Oh, yuk *her*!" Then the phone slammed down.

"Kenny, are you still there?"

"Yeah. It's just Monster-Sister listening in. She's gone now."

"Listen, I'm worried about Lyndz and all this stupid diet talk. We've got to do something about it."

"Like what?"

"I don't know, but we've got to talk

some sense into her, tell her she doesn't need to diet. It's turning her into a right misery. We could tell her we like her just as she is. And try to get Fliss off the subject too."

"OK. We'll tell them tonight. I agree with you. Dieting's for idiots."

"You could lose a bit of weight," cut in Molly, "off your mouth!"

"You're dead, Molly! Frankie, I'm going. I've got to murder my sister."

"Call me if you need any help."

Sometimes I'd love a sister. But then I think to myself, I could end up with one like Kenny's sister Molly! Oh, boy. I am so lucky to be an only child. She is gruesome. We call her Molly the Monster. I'll tell you about her another time.

But back to the kitchen. After it had cooled, I put five slices of scrummy pizza in a plastic box. Then I packed up my sleepover kit and Dad drove me to Fliss's in the car.

"Have a great time," he said as he

dropped me off.

"Thanks, Dad."

But then he wound down the window and called after me, "Oh, and Frankie, try and get some sleep tonight."

"Yes, Dad."

Honestly! Do your mum and dad always go on about getting a good night's sleep? Mine do. I can't help it if I'm not a great sleeper. My grandma says it's because I've got such an active brain. She's probably right, because my head's always full of stuff that keeps me awake. My dad says, "Active brain, my foot! It's because she's so nosy; she's frightened she'll miss something if she closes her eyes." He's so cheeky to me.

But sleepovers are different anyway. Nobody sleeps at sleepovers! In fact, they ought to be called *stay-awake-all-night-overs*. That's what we try to do. But don't tell your mum and dad that or they won't let you go to one.

"I'll try," I called back. "It's the others,

they keep me awake." And I smiled and waved, as if four-cheese pizza wouldn't melt in my mouth.

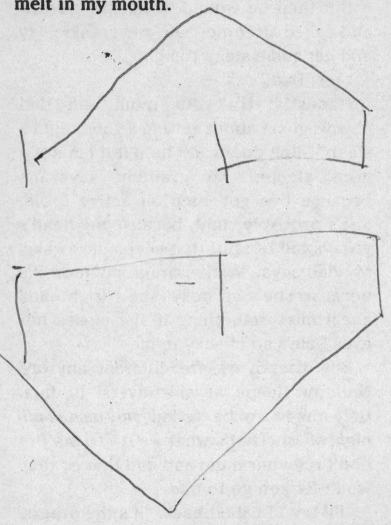

CHAPTER FOUR

When I rang the bell, Fliss's mum opened the door.

"Hello, Francesca. Take your shoes off, dear, and then you can go on up. Everyone else is here. Shall I take that box from you?"

"No, thanks, Mrs Sidebotham. It's just got a few bits of pizza in it."

"A few bits of pizza for a midnight feast, I'll bet," she said, smiling. "You'll try not to make a mess, won't you, sweetheart?"

I smiled and nodded. After all, we were going to eat it, not spread it on the carpet.

But as I've already told you, we have to be mega-careful at Fliss's house. I'd probably better tell you a bit about Fliss and her family next, then you'll understand why what happened later was such a D-for-disaster.

Fliss lives with her mum and her brother Callum – he's only seven and a bit of a pest – and Andy, her mum's boyfriend. Her dad lives just round the corner, with his girlfriend and her little boy and their new baby, Posie. She is so *cute*.

If you went to Fliss's house you would think she was dead posh, but she's not. It's just that her mum likes everything sparkly clean and neat and tidy. And cream! That's the other thing: everything's cream. The sofa, the curtains, even the carpet. So you have to take your shoes off the minute you go in. And you have to be on guard against spilling anything, or breaking anything, or scruffing anything up, unless you're in

Fliss's room or out in the garden. Then you can relax.

The lounge has got huge patio doors and the kitchen is like something in a TV ad. It's all shiny and new-looking and – you've guessed it – cream!

It's not a bit like my house. For a start, there are no piles of papers covering the table at Fliss's. No books, no newspapers all over the place. And no dog either.

Fliss would love a pet but the only one she's allowed is a goldfish called Bubbles. That's because goldfish don't leave hairs on the carpets. They don't do any other unmentionable things either! Well, I suppose they do but it just falls to the bottom of the bowl, until you clean it out.

Fliss's mum works at home. She does facials and massage and things. Fliss says she's a beauty technician. She also teaches keep-fit and aerobics. Andy is a plasterer. We don't see much of him because he works all the time.

The best thing about Fliss's house is

the whirlpool bath with its own Jacuzzi. It's ace. Guess what colour it is! No, you're wrong, actually. It's pink with gold taps.

The worst thing about Fliss's house is the people next door. The Grumpies.

That's what we call them. They're really called Charles and Jessica Watson-Wade and Baby Bruno. Honestly, I didn't make that up. Fliss's mum tries to be nice and get along with them but they're so stuck up and they're always complaining.

If Callum plays in the garden with his friends, it gives Mrs Watson-Wade a migraine.

If Fliss plays her tapes in her bedroom, it wakes Baby Bruno up.

If Andy doesn't cut the front hedge, it spoils the view from their lounge window.

They are seriously horrible.

So one of our hobbies, when we go to Fliss's, is winding up the Watson-Wades.

Sometimes we spy on them through a hole in the fence. Mrs Grumpy is mad about sunbathing and in the summer Fliss once saw her with nothing on. Well, that's what *she* said, but you can't believe everything Fliss tells you.

Lately, though, we've been annoying Mr Grumpy by setting off his car alarm. We got away with it the first few times, but last time he knew it was us and gave us this big lecture. He told us we were very naughty girls and we'd probably grow up to be vandals. We'd only set his car alarm off!

The Grumpies have got this *perfect* garden and *perfect* pond with dead-expensive carp in it. Mr Grumpy's always fishing out the leaves and the weeds. He even cuts the grass round it with a pair of scissors. We've seen him. He's always bragging about how it's his pride and joy. So we roll up bus tickets and sweet papers and push them through the hole in the fence, hoping they'll land in the pond on the other side. Then we watch him fishing them out. You can see him frowning, wondering where they've come from. We have to keep really quiet so he won't hear us laughing. Otherwise we'd get another lecture.

But we did something much worse than that this time. Oh, it was brilliant. They're never going to forgive us. No way. We're in serious doom with the Grumpies now.

After Fliss's mum let me in, I went upstairs and found the others all sitting on Fliss's bed. There were sleeping bags all over the room and plastic boxes of food and everybody's sleepover kits. I could only just get in.

"Hi, Frankie," said Kenny. "Show us what you've brought."

"The Authentic Thomas Four-Cheese Pizza," I said, opening the lid.

"Mmmm!" said Kenny. "Smells heavenly." *Heavenly* is Kenny's favourite word.

"Four-cheese!" said Fliss. "Do you realise how many calories that is?"

"Oh, don't start," I warned her.

She just shrugged and looked away.

"I brought flapjack," said Kenny. "My gran's recipe."

"Brown-sugar flapjack. Oh, Kenny, all those calories!" I said, grinning.

"Rosie's brought cheese straws," said Kenny.

"More cheese," Fliss muttered.

"What about you?" I asked Lyndz.

But Fliss spoke for her. "Lyndz has made popcorn and I've made a lemon surprise."

Well, that sounded OK. But all this talk about food was making me hungry. I didn't think I could wait till midnight.

"Why don't we have some now?" I suggested.

"You know the rules," said Fliss.

Fliss is pretty bossy most of the time, and when the sleepover's at her house there's no living with her. She's very strict about rules.

One of our rules is that we save our food until we're all in bed and it's dark.

We hardly ever manage to wait until midnight. But we try not to eat it too early.

"Anyway," she said, "I was just showing Rosie my room."

Uh-oh. Bor-ing. The grand tour of Fliss's bedroom was about to start.

CHAPTER FIVE

Rosie had never been to Fliss's house before because she was new to the Sleepover Club, so Fliss *had* to show her everything: all her ornaments, all her soft toys and the entire contents of her wardrobe. Fliss's got loads of clothes. I could see she was in a real showing-off mood, trying to impress Rosie. Not only has she got a lot of clothes, they're all hanging up or folded neatly, arranged according to colour. Sweaters, T-shirts, leggings, skirts, all colour-coordinated, and her shoes and boots lined up in pairs.

It looks like Sindy's wardrobe.

"Do you want to wear something of mine?" Fliss asked.

"Can I?" said Rosie, her eyes nearly popping out.

"I don't mind," said Fliss. "Anybody can borrow anything they like."

Well, she knows I'm too tall to get into anything of hers and Kenny only wears her Leicester City football shirt anyway. But Rosie borrowed her Ton-Sur-Ton tracksuit. It just fitted her because it was a bit sloppy on Fliss.

Lyndsey had gone all quiet and was looking really miserable again. I knew what that was about. I started thinking about what my mum had said and what she expected me to do about it.

"Do *you* want to borrow anything?" Fliss asked Lyndz.

Lyndsey shook her head.

"You'll soon fit in them, if you keep to the diet," said Fliss smugly.

"I hope you're not seriously on a diet,"

I said. "Diets are bad for you."

"Diets are for idiots," said Kenny.

"It's not really a diet," she said, but she'd gone all pink, so we knew it was a bit of a porky pie.

"Well, it'd better not be," I said. "Your mum would go mad if she knew. Just because Fliss is thin, there's no reason why you should be. It's stupid wanting to look like someone else. We're all different. You should be happy with the way you are. My grandma says, 'Comparison is a useless exercise'."

"Ooo-er! Get her!" said Kenny. "Frankie swallowed a dictionary."

It was quite a little speech and everyone looked at me as if I'd had a brain transplant.

"It's all right for you, Frankie," said Lyndsey. "You're tall and thin."

"Look," I said. "D'you suppose I like being this tall? Sometimes it really gets on my wires. Don't you think I'd like to be the same size as the rest of you? But what's the point of whingeing about it? I'm tall. There's nothing I can do about it."

I was feeling dead hot and embarrassed. I just wanted a hole to open up in the floor and swallow me. But then Kenny started up and made everything OK.

"Yeah," said Kenny, "Frankie's right. We're all different. D'you suppose I like being this gorgeous? Don't you think sometimes I'd like to be dead plain and ugly like the rest of you? It isn't easy being stunningly beautiful, you know. But I am. There's nothing I can do about that."

She was pulling stupid faces and posing, as if she was being photographed for *Just Seventeen*. Sometimes Kenny is so embarrassing she really makes us squeal. This was one of those times. She even made Lyndsey smile.

"You are too crazy to live," I said. And we set on her with our pillows.

"Oh, be careful!" said Fliss. "You might break something."

Well, she was right. Her room's pretty small and there isn't room to swing a cat, never mind a squishy-poo. A squishy-poo, by the way, is a sleeping bag filled with clothes and things so it makes a sort of *humungous* pillow for whacking people with. But before we could make one, Fliss said, "Let's go into the garden."

So we all got up and headed off downstairs for a round of International Gladiators on Fliss's back lawn.

"Don't make too much noise and annoy the neighbours," Fliss's mum called out from the lounge. "You know what they're like."

"Yes, Mum," Fliss called back. And we all grinned. We knew exactly what they were like. The Gruesome Grumpies.

Fliss's garden is dead neat and tidy, just like her house. We're allowed on the lawn, but we're not supposed to go on the flowerbeds, which is a bit of a problem when you're having *barging contests*.

This is what we do: first we get into pairs. One of us is the horse and the other's the rider. If you're the rider, you have to hold on tight and concentrate on staying on. If you're the horse, you have to barge into the other horse and try to push it off the grass. You can't use your hands *at all* and kicking is *not* allowed. Whoever's left out has to be the referee and see that nobody breaks the rules and decide who's the winner.

Actually it's not my favourite contest. Because I'm so much bigger than the others, I never get to be a rider. Kenny's a good sport and she did try once or twice to carry me but she just buckled at the knees and fell over.

So I was the horse and Kenny was my rider and Fliss was on Lyndz's back and they were wobbling all over the place. Rosie told us to get ready because she was about to blow her whistle. And then we were off.

You have to dodge, like you do in

netball, which I'm ace at, and so I soon had Lyndz in the rose bushes. It's always the same really, a push-over. A barge-over, come to think of it. Good joke?

First we did the best of three, but the other team complained so much that we did the best of five. In the end, we did the best of fifteen and Kenny and I still won. Ea-sy! Just at the end I caught up with Lyndsey against the fence and barged her right up against it. Fliss and Kenny started wrestling, which is not really allowed but we'd already won, so it didn't seem to matter. It was lucky the fence was there because they both lost their balance and had to grab hold of it. But then they wouldn't let go. They were so interested in what was going on in next door's garden, we couldn't get them to move.

"Will you let go and come down?" Lyndz was yelling at Fliss.

"I'm dropping you if you don't," I threatened Kenny.

But they wouldn't take any notice of us, so we dumped them in the flower bed. They were both giggling so much neither of them could speak.

Than a man's very cross face appeared over the fence.

"Felicity, has your mother never taught you it's very rude to snoop and stare at people in the privacy of their own garden?"

Fliss just looked down and mumbled, "Sorry."

Kenny was nearly wetting herself.

"Well, I shall have to speak to her about this and the appalling noise you've been making. You're like a pack of wild animals."

And then the man's face disappeared and we all fled into the house like a... pack of wild animals, actually.

CHAPTER SIX

We couldn't wait to get back into Fliss's bedroom. We were dying to laugh. We rolled around the bed shrieking.

"Snoop and stare!"

"How could you snoop and stare?"

"Have you no manners?"

"What are you, wild animals?"

"He is seriously weird," said Kenny.

"But what was he doing?" I said.

"I don't know," said Kenny, "but whatever it was, he looked so stupid."

"He was standing there in his pyjamas," said Fliss, "doing these funny movements with his arms and legs."

"Like this," said Kenny, and she gave us a demonstration that looked like a robot.

Then we heard the front doorbell ring and we all hid our faces in our pillows and did a bit of silent screaming. The next thing we knew, Fliss's mum was coming upstairs. We quickly pulled ourselves together, all except Kenny. When Kenny starts, it's impossible for her to stop. And by now Lyndsey had got hiccups, as usual. So those two rushed out and escaped to the bathroom.

Fliss's mum was shaking her head and looking quite worried. We all felt guilty when we saw her face.

"Mr Watson-Wade's just been round to complain that you've been laughing at him while he was trying to do his Tai Chi."

"Tai Chi?" said Fliss. "What's that?"

"It's sort of exercises, movements; it's Chinese, I think. I don't know, but he says you have to be quiet and concentrate very hard while you're doing it and you girls completely disturbed him. It's supposed to be relaxing."

"Is that why he was wearing his pyjamas?" said Felicity.

"I've no idea, but I've apologised and I think tomorrow, Felicity, you had better go round and apologise yourself. I've told you about upsetting the neighbours."

Fliss just looked down and pulled a face. I didn't dare look at Rosie or I would have started off again. Rosie was sucking her thumb. I'd never seen her do that before but she said afterwards it was the only way she could stop herself from laughing.

"I think you'd better get ready for bed now."

"Aw, Mum, it's not very late," said Fliss.

"It's gone nine and I know you girls, by the time you're in bed it'll be gone ten. So I think you'd better start getting ready now."

Fliss's mum was right. It *was* gone ten

before we were in bed, because we do so much fooling around. At home I can get ready for bed in four minutes flat. I've timed it.

Starting from... now! Clothes off... and that's thirty seconds.

Pyjamas on and into the bathroom... and that's one minute gone.

Wet the flannel and a quick face and hands wipe... another thirty seconds. It takes a minute if you bother with the full soap treatment.

Then the slow bit: cleaning your teeth. Cap off the tube, quick squirt and brush, brush, brush, brush, brush, top and bottom. Gargle, gargle, quick spit out, dry your mouth... that's another minute gone.

Then leap on the loo... thirty seconds or a minute, depending on you know what.

Race back and leap into bed. Four minutes on the button!

When we're having a sleepover, things take a bit longer. Getting undressed, for a start. We always get undressed inside our sleeping bags. We *can* do it in two minutes, maybe a bit longer for me because I nearly fill the sleeping bag with my long arms and legs. But we usually take longer because we do this sort of invisible striptease. We wriggle down so we can't see each other and then we take off our clothes and throw them out at each other, especially our smelly socks. It's a great laugh.

We also spend a lot of time queueing to get into the bathroom and arguing about whose turn it is and waiting behind the bedroom door with a squishy-poo for whoever's last to come back.

Fliss was in her bed, Lyndz was in the spare bed, Rosie and Kenny and I were in a row in our sleeping bags on the floor between them. It was fine as long as the ones in the beds didn't try to get out of bed and step on our heads, and as long as the three of us didn't keep turning over and squashing each other.

Fliss's mum came in to say good night to us. "Have you girls got enough room there?"

"Yeah, we're fine," we told her.

"As snug as a bug," said Kenny.

"It's ever so late. I hope I'm not going to get into trouble with your mums," she said.

"Don't worry, Mrs Sidebotham. I never go to sleep at home before this time," I told her. "I'm a really late bird."

"You're a cuckoo," said Kenny. So I thumped her.

"Now settle down, girls," said Fliss's mum. She always has this worried look, so we did. She turned off the main light and closed the door. We lay very quiet and counted slowly to twenty until we were sure she'd gone and then we got our torches out.

"OK," said Rosie, "what are we going to do now?".

"Isn't it time to eat yet?" said Kenny.

"I'm ravenous."

"We've only just got into bed," said Fliss. "Let's have a game first. Or a story."

"But I'm starving," said Kenny.

"So am I," I said.

"Me too," said Rosie.

Lyndz said nothing, she just looked quiet, not a bit how she usually is. But the main thing was, Fliss was outvoted.

We all reached over and got out our food boxes. We passed them round and took a piece out of each. Well, Rosie and Kenny and I did. Fliss refused any pizza, she turned her nose up at the flapjack and she broke half a cheese straw off.

Lyndz was about to take her piece when she saw Fliss watching her. She just shook her head.

"Where's your popcorn?" I said.

Lyndz passed her box over.

"Great," said Kenny, until she saw it. "There's no sugar on this."

"Fewer calories," said Fliss.

Kenny passed it back without taking any.

Then Fliss passed a plastic bowl over. "Have some lemon surprise. It's out of the Weight Watchers cookbook. It's only twenty-five calories a portion."

"It tastes like lemon Jif," said Kenny, screwing up her face and almost spitting it out.

"Please yourself," said Fliss, eating some herself and then passing it to Lyndz.

Lyndz passed it back. "I'm not really hungry."

I was. Kenny and I had eaten our pieces of pizza *and* our flapjack *and* our cheese straws. In the end we even ate some of Lyndz's dry popcorn. We didn't eat any lemon Jif, thank you very much. We weren't that hungry.

I looked at the two pieces of pizza left in the box, but it seemed too greedy to eat those as well. I put the top back on the box, so it wouldn't be too tempting.

"What time is it?" asked Lyndsey.

"It's just gone eleven o'clock."

"What shall we do now?" I said.

"Tell us a story, Frankie," said Rosie.

"It'll have to be a short one," said Lyndsey. "I'm dead tired."

"A scary one," said Kenny.

"No, not a scary one," said Fliss. She hadn't got over the last time, when we'd scared ourselves silly talking to ghosts after Lyndz's birthday sleepover.

"I know," said Kenny. "Let's tell jokes. I'll go first, I've got a really good one. Why was the patient's cough better the next morning? Because he'd been practising all night."

"Shall I tell you the joke about the butter?" said Rosie. "I'd better not, you'll only spread it."

"Me next," I said. "Knock, knock."

"Who's there?"

"Howard."

"Howard who?"

"Howard you like to be outside for a change?"

Everybody groaned, but I'd got lots more like that.

"Knock, knock."
"Who's there?"
"Boo!"
"Boo-hoo?"
"Don't cry, it's only a joke."

CHAPTER SEVEN

I could have kept it up for hours but we heard Fliss's mum coming. We switched off our torches and lay with our eyes closed, pretending to be asleep. Kenny even did a bit of heavy breathing, which made us all start to giggle.

"Oh, dear, are you still awake?" she whispered. "You'll never be able to wake up tomorrow and I'll be in trouble with your mums. Now, please, settle down and go to sleep, there's good girls."

Then she went out and closed the door. But we still hadn't sung our going-to-sleep song, so we sat up in the torchlight and sang dead quietly, almost whispering:

"Down by the river there's a hanky-pankyyy,

With a bull-frog sitting near the hanky-pankyyy.

With an ooh-ahh, ooh-ahh, hey, Mrs Zippy, with a 1-2-3- OUT!"

We didn't sit up and do the actions. Everyone was too tired by now. Except me; I was still wide awake. I could hear Lyndz sucking her thumb and Fliss sniffing and Rosie wriggling about trying to get comfy. But I couldn't settle down.

I was feeling hungry. I know I'd had quite a lot to eat but I felt a bit like Winnie the Pooh. There was this little corner and I needed to fill it. I'd probably have been OK if I hadn't known there were two pieces of scrummy pizza just a few centimetres away. I could hear them calling my name.

You don't have to look at me like that. I'm not proud of it, but I just couldn't help myself. And they *were* mine, in a way. After all, I made them. Anyway, I ate them.

I heard midnight striking and then at last I fell asleep.

OK, let's sit down for a bit on this bench and I'll finish the story off before we get to Kenny's. Otherwise she'll start chipping in and spoiling it. And if any of the others are round at hers, they'll join in too.

When I woke up it was still dark, so for a minute I wasn't sure whether I'd been asleep at all. Lyndz had her hand on my shoulder and was whispering to me, "Frankie, are you awake?"

Then I realised I had been asleep but not for very long. It wasn't morning yet. It was starting to get light but it was very quiet so it must have been early. I turned over to face her and rubbed my eyes.

"I'm starving," she said. "Can I have my pizza now?"

I was glad Lyndz had come to her senses and wanted to eat again, but now I felt so guilty. I'd eaten both pieces of pizza and I felt a real pig.

"It's all gone," I whispered. "I'm sorry." And I really was.

"Gone where?" she whispered back.

But I didn't want to go into that, so I said. "Have some flapjack instead." I reached behind Kenny's head for her plastic box. It felt suspiciously light when I picked it up.

Yeah, you guessed right. That little porker had eaten the spare flapjack as well.

"Oh, no!" said Lyndz, when I showed her. "I'm so hungry."

By now I was wide awake and feeling I ought to do something about it, but I couldn't think what. I rolled over and shook Kenny and whispered in her ear, "Lyndz is starving, pass it on."

"What are you talking about, you mad woman?" said Kenny, as if it was part of her dream.

"It's your fault, you ate the flapjack, you little porker," I whispered. "Now pass it on."

So Kenny rolled over, shook Rosie, and whispered, "Lyndz is ravenous. Pass it on."

Rosie rubbed her eyes and whispered, "What time is it?"

"Never mind what time it is," hissed Kenny. "Just pass the cheese straws."

Rosie's face went bright pink. This can't be true, I thought, but it was.

"I ate them," she whispered.

"I don't believe it," said Kenny. She turned and whispered to me, "She ate them!"

"Well, tell her to pass it on," I whispered back.

So Rosie knelt up and shook Fliss. "Lyndz is dying of hunger."

Fliss groaned and turned over but Rosie kept shaking her until she sat up.

"Can't she eat the leftovers?" Fliss

63

hissed at us.

"There aren't any," I said. "And no, she doesn't want lemon Jif for breakfast."

By now we were all wide awake.

"What time is it?" said Fliss.

I turned on my torch and read my watch. "Half past four."

"Half past four! I can't wake my mum up at this time."

"Can't you go and get me something out of the fridge?" said Lyndz.

"Oh, honestly! I'm not your servant, you know." That is another thing about Fliss, she's very grumpy when she wakes up. "It's not my fault you're hungry."

"Well, it is, actually," I said.

"How d'you make that out?"

"If you hadn't got her started on this stupid diet stuff in the first place, she'd have had her pizza and flapjack and cheese straws while they were still there to eat. And she wouldn't be hungry now."

"So where are they? Who ate them?"

Rosie and Kenny and I put up our hands, as if we were at school.

"You are such pigs," said Fliss.

We all grunted in chorus.

"Well, aren't *you* hungry? You didn't have much either," Lyndz asked her.

Fliss went pink. "A bit."

"We're all hungry, actually," said Rosie.

"We need *food*," said Kenny.

Fliss got out of bed. "OK, but we'll have to be quiet. If we wake my mum and Andy, there'll be big trouble. Come on."

So we all tiptoed down the stairs and into the kitchen.

Rosie hadn't been in Fliss's kitchen yet, so she was really impressed with that as well. "This is amazing!" she said. "It's so new... and shiny... and modern! You should see mine. It's like something out of the Dark Ages. My mum would go wild if she saw this. You are so lucky."

Now there is nothing Fliss likes better than people telling her things like that.

"It's not new," she said. "We've had it for ages."

"Oh, and look! You've got a waffle-maker."

The truth is, Fliss's mum is mad on gadgets and every time we go there's something new. You name it, she's got it.

"Oh, can we have waffles?" Rosie begged. "Please. They're scrummy."

I thought Fliss would just go to the fridge and get us a yoghurt or make a sandwich or something. Not on your life. Fliss was determined to impress everyone, Rosie especially. She put on her mum's apron and said, "Right, what do the rest of you want?" Just as if she was taking orders in McDonald's.

"Porridge."

"Toast."

"Milkshake."

"OK," she said.

"Can you really do all that?" said Lyndz.

"Seriously?" said Rosie. "Are you allowed?"

"Yeah," said Fliss. "My mum lets me do anything in the kitchen."

"Even waffles?" I said, suspiciously.

"We-ell, the waffle-maker's new. I'm not so sure about that."

"I can do waffles," said Kenny. "My auntie's got one."

"I can do the toast," said Lyndz. "Where's the bread?"

"I'll do the milkshakes," said Rosie.

Soon they were all racing round the kitchen, opening cupboards, in and out of the fridge. I sat on one of the high bar stools, watching. To tell you the truth, I was feeling a bit icky. Not exactly sick, you know, just a bit, urghhh. But old Bossy-boots spotted me.

"Don't just sit there, Frankie," she said. "You set the table."

"OK." I slid down and started to search for table mats and cutlery and ketchup and anything else I could think of. If we were going to have a party, we might as well have a proper one.

For my Brownie Hostess badge I'd had to lay a table and make a table decoration. I found some candlesticks and I looked round for something else I could use. I thought I'd better not ask Fliss; everyone else was already firing questions at her.

"Where's the salt?"

"Can I use these bananas?"

"Is this the only milk you've got?"

"Haven't you got any sliced bread?"

"I don't know," she snapped back. "You'll have to look. I can't do everything." She was getting in a razz because she'd spilled porridge oats all over the table. I tried to help her but she said, "I can manage. I've done this lots of times, you know."

So I tried to help Rosie with the milkshakes. She let me slice a banana, big deal! But then she said *she* wanted to do the mixing. So I watched Lyndz have three attempts at cutting a slice of bread. Every time she ended up with a wedge that looked like a dry ski slope and a pile of breadcrumbs you could have stuffed a mattress with.

"Oh, go away, Frankie! It's because you're watching me. You're putting me off."

So I watched Kenny instead, whisking this mixture of eggs and milk so fast most of it shot up in the air and all over the worktop.

"Look out!" I said.

"Look out yourself," she said. "Give me some room, can't you?"

"Keep your voices down," Fliss whispered above the noise. "You'll wake everyone."

Just then we heard footsteps on the stairs. We all stopped what we were doing and tried to hide things behind our backs. We stood still and froze to the spot, watching the kitchen door handle turn, expecting to see Fliss's mum's face or, even worse, Andy's. We were madly trying to think of a good excuse.

But when the door opened, it was Callum, Fliss's little brother, otherwise known as the Pest, standing in the doorway. He was rubbing his eyes and yawning. "What're you lot doing?" he said.

We all let out a sigh and relaxed. The worst danger was over. Now we just had to deal with him.

CHAPTER EIGHT

Fliss rushed over and dragged Callum into the kitchen and closed the door behind him. "Shhh! Keep your voice down," she hissed at him. "You're not supposed to be up at this time."

"Neither are you."

"You'll get into trouble if Mum and Andy wake up."

"So will you."

"What do you want, anyway?"

His eyes travelled round the kitchen. "I'm hungry."

"Join the club," said Lyndsey.

"All right, sit down and don't move," said Fliss. "We'll make you some breakfast if you swear you'll keep quiet and behave."

"You know I'm not allowed to swear."

"Oh, very funny," said Fliss, in a tired voice. "Just sit there and stay out of our way." Then she went back to the porridge preparations.

I sat opposite Callum and watched him. I've often wanted a sister but I've never really wanted a brother, especially a younger brother like Callum.

"What're you staring at?" he said.

"I don't know," I said, "the label's fallen off."

"Get me a drink," he said and, like an idiot, I did.

After that, since everyone else was busy slicing and chopping and stirring and slopping things in all directions and wouldn't let me join in, I thought I'd go out into the garden to pick a few flowers to make the table look nice.

Quick, the toaster's on fire!

I went to the back door but there was no key in the lock. I looked everywhere I could think it might be: on a hook, like at my house, on a shelf, in a drawer in the hall stand. But it wasn't there. So I went back into the kitchen to ask Fliss.

In those few moments I'd been gone, the kitchen had turned into a disaster area. The thick chunk of toast that Lyndz had cut was now stuck in the toaster and smoke was coming out of it. Luckily we'd all done our Home Safety badge.

"Turn it off!" squealed Fliss.

"At the plug!" we all squealed together.

"I know, I know," she squealed back.

But the smoke had set off the smoke alarm and now it was flashing and pinging.

"Someone wave a newspaper at it," said Fliss. "Quick, before it wakes my mum."

Fliss was busy watching her porridge frothing in the microwave, so I grabbed a magazine and waved it in the air until the alarm went silent.

For a couple of seconds everything was quiet. I was just about to ask Fliss where the back-door key was kept when Kenny let out a cry. I'd watched her pouring the mixture into the waffle-maker and I'd thought it looked sort of thin. Now it was running down the sides and all over the work surface and down the cupboard doors. A little pool on the floor at her feet was already turning into a river.

"Look what you're doing!" squealed Fliss. "Get a cloth and clear it up."

"Where will I find one?" said Kenny.

"I'll get it," I said, rushing to the sink at exactly the same moment Fliss bent to get one out of the cupboard. We banged heads.

"Oh, thanks very much," she shouted at me.

"It was an accident," I shouted back.

But there was no time to worry about the small matter of two cracked skulls because by now Fliss's porridge was bubbling over the side of the bowl and frothing all over the microwave. It reminded me of that bit in *Gremlins* when one of the gremlins gets put in the microwave. Gruesome.

"Oh no! Now look what you've made me do!" Fliss screamed at Kenny.

"*I* made you do?" Kenny screamed back.

This could have turned into a **big** one, but just then another disaster struck.

Rosie had been having a great time chopping loads of fruit: apples and raisins and a few nuts she'd found in the cupboard. In fact, anything she could lay her hands on. She'd poured a whole bottle of milk into the liquidiser and was ready to turn it on. She was sniffing the mixture, which looked and smelt delicious. And it would have been, I'm sure, if she'd had the sense to put the lid on properly.

Unfortunately, she didn't. Right in the middle of Fliss and Kenny's argument, the liquidiser lid flew up in the air and hit the fridge door. Milkshake hit the room at fifty miles an hour, most of it landing on Rosie. It coated her hair and face so that she looked like something out of *Gremlins* too.

"Oh, my God, what have you done?" Fliss shrieked at Rosie.

"Boy, are you gonna be in trouble when my mum sees this," said Callum. The little toad was grinning from ear to ear.

"Shut up!" Fliss hissed at him. "Just get it all cleaned up now," she yelled at the rest of us.

I'd already tried to help Kenny clean up the waffle mess but she'd just pushed me out of the way. And now Fliss was giving Rosie a big lecture, so I thought, OK, I'm out of here. They can all do their own cleaning-up. I hadn't made any of the mess. It wasn't my fault.

So I went out into the hall and suddenly had this brainwave. I thought, I can get into the garden through the patio doors in the lounge. So I did. And that was the reason I wasn't around when Kenny had her accident – can you believe it, I *still* managed to get the blame for it.

I heard all about it afterwards, a dozen times at least, so I can tell you exactly what happened. And I suppose Fliss was right, it wouldn't have happened if I'd stayed in the kitchen.

All the time the liquidiser was throwing milkshake over Rosie's head, and the porridge was erupting in the microwave, and the waffle mixture was running down the cupboards, Lyndz was trying to toast a second slab of toast and, surprise, surprise, that got stuck as well. This time the toaster smoked even worse and a couple of flames came out of it.

"Turn it off!" Fliss squealed again.

"At the plug!" Rosie and Kenny joined in.

But this time it had caused so much smoke that even though they all waved newspapers and magazines in the air, the smoke alarm wouldn't stop. That's why I got the blame. None of them was tall enough to reach the alarm, so it went on pinging and flashing.

"Now you're going to be for it," said Callum again.

Well, Fliss nearly went haywire. "Shut up!" she shouted at him. "Just shut up! Oh, please, can't somebody make that stop?" she begged the others.

So Kenny jumped up on one of the bar stools, taking swipes at it with a magazine.

"Die, you alien!" she said, swiping furiously.

"Oh, stop fooling around, Kenny," said Lyndz.

"She's going to fall in a minute," said Rosie.

"Oh, where's Frankie, for goodness' sake?" yelled Fliss.

CHAPTER NINE

Good question! Well, in fact, at exactly that same moment, after a lot of fiddling, I had just managed to unlock the patio door. This turned out to be a *big* mistake and was the second reason I got the blame for everything, even though I wasn't there.

This dreadful noise started up and I nearly died. No, it wasn't the smoke alarm. That was gentle and quite soothing compared with this din. This was the burglar alarm. I'd set it off opening the patio doors.

I didn't know what to do. I tried closing the door again but it didn't make any difference. It still went on blaring away.

I mean, what would you have done? I didn't know whether to close the door, sneak back in the kitchen and pretend it had nothing to do with me, or rush out into the garden and find somewhere to hide. So I was stuck there, half in and half out, like a burglar in the middle of a smash-and-grab raid that's gone wrong.

Back in the kitchen things were even worse. Perhaps it was the shock of hearing the burglar alarm that panicked Kenny. Whatever it was, she took one big swipe at the smoke alarm and fell off the stool. Lyndz tried to catch her, missed, and they both landed on the floor in a heap with Kenny's arm underneath them.

And then everyone went to pieces. They could hear the burglar alarm blaring away and now they could hear the sound of Fliss's mum and Andy getting out of bed.

"Uh-oh," said Callum, looking like the cat that's got the cream. "Trouble."

Standing there with the porridge bowl in her hands, Fliss took one look around the kitchen. There was a smell of burning again, but this time it wasn't the toaster, it was coming from the waffle-maker. When Rosie opened it, out popped four rubber waffles.

There were already two fat rounds of black toast on the worktop that were so burnt you could have played football with them.

"What am I going to do?" Fliss whimpered. "They'll go mad."

Lyndz was trying to help Kenny up. By now she'd realised it wasn't just a bit of a bump they'd had and she could see Kenny's arm was really hurting. Fliss was in shock and Callum was no use whatsoever. So that only left Rosie. Luckily she took charge.

She grabbed the rubber waffles and the burnt toast and dumped them in the porridge bowl and charged out of the kitchen with them. She rushed into the hall just as I was coming back in.

"Where are you going?" I asked her.

"Quick," she said. "We've got to get rid of the evidence."

"Into the garden," I said. "This way." And I led her out through the patio doors. The noise was even worse outside.

"What's going on?" I shouted.

"Someone set off the alarm," she shouted back at me.

Even then I could see how funny we must look, both standing there in our pyjamas, shouting at each other and holding all this burnt food. Suddenly we saw Fliss's mum and Andy through the kitchen window so we ducked round the corner out of sight.

"What are we going to do with this?" said Rosie, holding the bowl out in front of her.

Now, I know the sensible thing would have been to dump it all in the dustbin, but the dustbin was round the other side of the house and we didn't dare go past the windows in case they saw us. And anyway, at half past five in the morning I wasn't feeling very sensible.

"Oh, Frankie, what are we going to do with it?" Rosie said again.

Why is it that people always expect me to come up with ideas?

Yeah, yeah, I know. Because I always do.

We were standing close to the next door's fence, so, without thinking much about it, I flung the two burnt slabs of toast over the fence into the Grumpies' garden and then threw the waffles after them.

"What are you doing?" Rosie shrieked. I just grinned. I thought it was a neat idea.

Now we were just left with the bowl of porridge. This wasn't ordinary porridge that you can pour out of a pan, this was Fliss's specially constructed quick-set cement porridge. You'd have needed a knife and fork to eat it. So I just turned the bowl upside down and it fell on the grass in a solid ball.

For a second Rosie stood looking at it. Then she started grinning too. She picked it up and hurled it over the fence after the toast and waffles.

We suddenly realised that it had all gone quiet. The alarm had been turned off.

I was still holding the bowl when Fliss's mum came through the patio doors.

"Come in, this minute!" she called. "You'll catch your death of cold."

And that was the first time we noticed that it really was freezing.

When we got in, we soon realised we'd only got rid of some of the evidence. There was plenty more of it left in the kitchen. But nobody seemed to bother much about the mess, they were far more worried about Kenny's accident.

Poor old Kenny was a funny grey colour by the time we got in. Andy strapped up her arm before he took her to the hospital. I couldn't work out for the life of me how you could get a broken arm just making waffles. Rosie gave me the full story while we were sitting in Casualty waiting for Kenny to have her arm set.

Fliss and her mum and Lyndz stayed at home to look after Callum and do the clearing-up. Andy took me and Rosie with him to Leicester Infirmary, because it was still only six o'clock and too early to deliver us home on a Sunday morning.

I couldn't believe so much had happened in only an hour. We all sat as quiet as mice in the car. When the nurse called Kenny's name, Andy went in with her to get her arm X-rayed, because her mum and dad hadn't arrived yet. So then Rosie had the chance to tell me the bits I'd missed while I was busy breaking out of Fliss's house.

"But what were you doing to set the alarm off in the first place?" said Rosie.

"I was trying to pick some flowers," I said. And I knew as soon as I said it that it sounded a pathetic excuse.

It was half past eight before we got back from the hospital. Kenny's mum and dad had come to take her home. She was fine. She'd loved every minute of it. Kenny adores hospitals. She's weird that way. She's hurt her arm a couple of times before but never badly enough to have a plaster, so she was mega-excited and couldn't wait to go to school to get everyone to sign it.

We were just relieved it was all over. Because everyone had been so worried about Kenny, we'd not really been told off much... until we got back to Fliss's! When we saw her mum's face, we could tell there was plenty to come. Boy, was she in a razz!

GOODBYE

Andy had been quite good fun on the way back in the car. He was starting to tease us about trying to get us on these new TV programmes: *Ready Steady, Wreck the Kitchen* and *Can't Cook, Better Not Cook Ever Again* and silly things like that. So we all went into the house smiling.

Fliss tried to warn us. She waved her hands nervously at us from behind her mum, who stood in the kitchen doorway with her arms folded and a cross expression on her face. They must have worked hard because the kitchen was back to normal. It was all smart and shiny and gleaming cream behind her.

Then she moved and beckoned us to follow. The only thing that was out of place and completely spoiled the effect was a tray sitting in the middle of the worktop with two large slabs of burnt toast on it and four rubber waffles and a football made out of porridge. The only difference between now and the last time we'd seen them was that then they were dry and now they were soaking wet.

"Mr Watson-Wade has just been round," she said, talking between her teeth. "And brought these with him. It seems he fished them out of his pond. I don't suppose either of you two happens to know how they got there?"

Sometimes honesty is *definitely* the best policy. We just came clean and owned up. We got a serious earwigging from Fliss's mum. Kenny got off lightest, because of her arm. Fliss got into most trouble because it seems she is definitely not allowed, no way, under no circumstances, to do any cooking whatsoever without her mum there to supervise. Well, that was news to us! She was banned from cooking *for ever*. Or at least until her mum forgets about it, which won't be soon.

Of course, when the rest of our parents heard the story, they all said the same thing, more or less, so that puts all of us out of the Brownie competition.

But the good news is Lyndz has stopped talking about stupid diets. She was sick of it anyway and now she's back to her old self, with her smily face and her happy knees, and we're all glad about that.

Fliss has learnt her lesson too. She never talks about diets any more either, we've cured her of that. Whenever she mentions it, we all start yawning and tell her she's really bor-ing. Now we have great midnight feasts again and sleepovers are back to normal. Thank goodness!

At first Fliss and I had a mega-row when she tried to make out it had all been my fault. She said that if I hadn't made her feel guilty, she'd never have taken us down to the kitchen. And if I hadn't gone out of the kitchen, I'd have been there to stop the smoke alarm, and if I'd been in the kitchen with the rest of them, I couldn't have been in the lounge setting off the burglar alarms and waking up her mum and Andy and getting us all caught.

That's her side of the story. This is mine: if she hadn't started Lyndz on this stupid diet, we'd all have had plenty to eat, Lyndz wouldn't have woken up in the middle of the night starving, we wouldn't have gone down into the kitchen, Fliss wouldn't have started showing off and pretending she could cook things she couldn't, we wouldn't have had any disasters and Rosie and I wouldn't have needed to dispose of the evidence. So there, now you've heard both sides and you can decide.

Oh, look! Lyndz's bike is outside Kenny's house so that means she's there. You'll be able to meet her at last. And Kenny might let you sign her plaster. Just your name, mind, no rude jokes; she's already got into trouble for that. She let Ryan Scott write on it at school. I did warn her. But that's Kenny for you. Completely barmy.

Come on, let's go in. I can't wait for you to meet them.

Mega Sleepover Club ②

Fliss is desperate for a pet in *The Sleepover Club at Rosie's*, and volunteers to look after the school hamster for the weekend. Oh-oh... Kenny's horrible sister is out to make trouble in *The Sleepover Club at Kenny's* – have the Sleepover Club met their match? And in *Starring the Sleepover Club*, it's all fun and games with Fliss's mum's camcorder. Will the Sleepover Club discover screen stardom, or will their film be a flop?

**Three fantastic Sleepover Club
stories in one!**

www.harpercollinschildrensbooks.co.uk

Mega Sleepover Club ③

The gang decide to form a pop group in *The Sleepover Girls go Spice*, except their secret rehearsal in the attic doesn't quite go to plan... *The 24-Hour Sleepover Club* sees the mates at loggerheads with their dreaded rivals, the M&Ms – and they soon find that revenge can be sickly sweet! And make way for chaos in *The Sleepover Club Sleeps Out*, when a school trip overnight to a local Egyptian museum provides a perfect excuse for terrifying the M&Ms...

Three fantastic Sleepover Club stories in one!

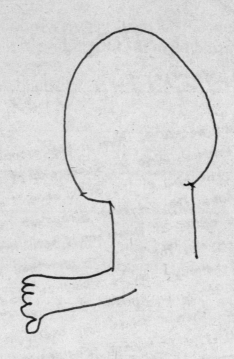

Order Form

To order direct from the publishers, just make a list of the titles you want and fill in the form below:

Name ...Mary....Kate..

Address ...5...clover...park...

....

....

Send to: Dept 6, HarperCollins Publishers Ltd, Westerhill Road, Bishopbriggs, Glasgow G64 2QT.

Please enclose a cheque or postal order to the value of the cover price, plus:

UK & BFPO: Add £1.00 for the first book, and 25p per copy for each additional book ordered.

Overseas and Eire: Add £2.95 service charge. Books will be sent by surface mail but quotes for airmail despatch will be given on request.

A 24-hour telephone ordering service is available to holders of Visa, MasterCard, Amex or Switch cards on 0141- 772 2281.

Collins
An *Imprint* of HarperCollins*Publishers*

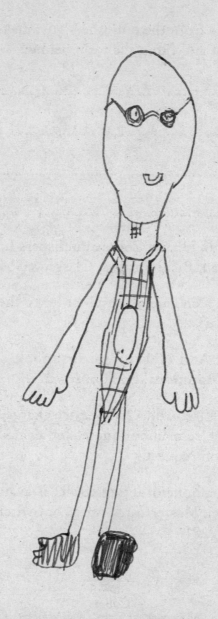